WHAT READERS ARE SAYING:

"Badass and brilliant."

"If Bond was a woman...and, like, 50 times sexier."

"Gritty and filled with tension—in and out of the bedroom."

"An evocative heroine in a savage plot."

COMING SOON:

Open Endings

In marriage, trust is everything.

2020

Hard TRIGGER

A ROGUE ROMANCE

S.L. HANNAH

CONCEPT
PUBLISHING

the adventures of hannah
CONCEPT PUBLISHING

Copyright © 2018 by S.L. Hannah

Published in the United States by The Adventures of Hannah–Concept Publishing.
www.theadventuresofhannah.com

Paperback ISBN 978-1-7323056-6-3
eBook ISBN 978-1-7323056-5-6

Printed in the United States of America

Editor: Jennifer Thomas
Associate Editor: Scott Frazelle
Text Design: The Adventures of Hannah
Cover Design: Cami Brite

First Paperback Edition

For Jennifer—
Thirteen years, six books...you're more than just my editing pen,
you're a good friend. Thank you for always pushing me.
I'm truly grateful, even when we're fighting about semicolons.

And to Dean & Anthony—
I know more about wielding guns than I ever thought I would.
Thank you for making it sound and feel real.

And to Lili & Walter—
For the crucial lessons in how to talk dirty, in Spanish. And how
to talk in Bajan slang. Gracias, amigos.

HARD TRIGGER

A ROGUE ROMANCE

LAS VEGAS

ONE

The door to the poker room shuts quietly behind me.

I take in a deep breath of the climatized air as I place one tall heel carefully in front of the other, sinking into the plush carpet of the casino floor. I pass by a wall of mirrors and catch my left heel, making a sudden stop…enough to be reminded of my bruised knee.

I fell on it, hard.

I place my palm against the reflective glass. Swollen knuckles make my fingers look like sausages. And there's dried blood on the gash over my thick eyebrow. *Damn, he got me good.* I should have had it stitched, but there wasn't time. There's rarely time in those situations. You think fast and hope you thought right, later. Besides, going to an ER or clinic…I'm sure that's the first place they went looking for me.

Yeah, but you should've covered it with makeup, I chide myself, wetting a finger and tracing the dark red trail of the wound. *You're getting sloppy.* The dealer asked me a couple of times if everything was alright. I poke at the bags under my bloodshot brown eyes. *God, I look thirty-three instead of twenty-three.*

I straighten and turn back for the catwalk up to the bar near the sports book.

It's a little after midnight on a Friday and the Wynn is buzzing in anticipation of the hot weekend ahead. Not just because of record temperatures for May, but because of the onslaught of conferences, concerts, and celebrities.

The leather seats at the video poker machines embedded in the glossy wood bar are nearly full, but I spy a vacancy between a Persian man who's more interested in the cigar he's smoking than the digital display he punches every now and then, and an Asian woman who maniacally navigates the buttons with gold-ringed fingers. Determined to win. Determination is all you have sometimes, especially in a town like this.

As I slide into the empty seat, I scan the area for anything out of the ordinary. Men who look like they're not in a casino to gamble…lingering stares…messages covertly conveyed… hidden weapons within reach. No one would dare touch me at a high-profile, tightly monitored place like this…but still.

I adjust the drape of my black silk dress as I cross my long legs, tanned from the sun. One hand habitually reaches into my clutch for the pack of Pall Malls I picked up before flying out of Mexico City to Las Vegas.

"What can I get you?" the bartender asks, clicking a lighter at the cigarette I've placed between my lips.

"Dirty martini," I reply, leaning into the flame. "Belvedere, four olives." I inhale slowly. "Very dirty," I add as the tobacco hits fast and my mind unwinds in time with my slow exhale from tonight's poker game.

I've never won this much. Especially on a bluff.

The bartender places an ashtray in front of me and smiles politely before turning for the stack of glasses.

I pull out a hundred from my wallet and work it into the machine in front of me, picking the progressive double bonus poker game. It has the best odds, they say. Regardless, it's a nice cool down to what has been a long evening of the real thing.

As I toy with the embroidered pattern on the front of my dress, I observe the couple across the bar from me. They're on their way to somewhere that doesn't matter because it's not their first date. He runs his fingers across her smooth chocolate-brown skin before dipping his mouth into hers. She wraps one hand around his sturdy neck, lunging deeper. The glimmer of the rock on her ring finger holds my stare.

I move my fingers up the skin of my neck, gulping down a lump of sorrow before turning toward my fresh martini.

Taking a long sip and tapping my cigarette against the ashtray, I curb my emotions and smack the Max Bet button.

Jacks or better.

I select the two jacks before drawing again. Two more jacks.

Winner.

The machine tallies my winnings of two hundred fifty dollars. I glance back at the couple, now sharing an intimate laugh between whispers in ears. *At least I can win at cards.* I press Max Bet again. The machine sets me up for a straight.

"They say a woman who sits alone at a video poker machine is looking to meet someone."

Slowly, I press four cards on the display in sequence and hit Deal. I'd recognize that voice in the most deafening environment. That deep, rumbling tone with just enough of an accent to distinguish that English is not his first language. My insides clench. The machine tallies up another twenty dollars.

My gaze shifts towards him. The temperature in my cheeks rises as my convictions crumble. I haven't seen or spoken to Diego Herrera since abruptly leaving him in a small seaside town on the Adriatic in Croatia a few weeks ago.

We'd decided to take a trip at the start of summer and landed in a place where not even a famous person would be recognized as anything more than a village-dweller. We'd satiated our cravings by barely leaving the old-world flat above the quaint café. It was far away from our complicated worlds and the most luxurious thing I've done in as long as I can remember. But then my stepfather called.

I told Diego that I had to leave immediately. We argued about everything—which soon stopped having to do with anything—and then I gave him back the ring he'd slid onto my finger just two nights prior.

The detached look on his face…

I didn't expect to see him again, maybe ever. Especially not tonight. But here he is in a white dress shirt, unbuttoned just enough to reveal his dense black chest hair. An undone bow tie hangs limply around his neck, accenting the cross he always wears, and his dark hair is greasy enough with product to stay off…*that face*. Chiseled to perfection yet marked by a few good fights if you look close enough.

If you can get close enough.

"What are you doing here, Diego?" I ask, inhaling from my cigarette.

A smirk creases his face. The scar he earned above his lip when we tried cliff-jumping in ninth grade stretches, distracting from those irresistible dimples.

"Poker."

He stops my hand before it can reach the Max Bet button again. I wince.

"And trying to stop you from making another mistake, Victoria."

Inspecting my swollen knuckles, his fingers press right on the spot where he placed that ring.

A ring that came without questions or presumptions. A ring that acknowledged the jarring interruption to our friendship when he was sent off to University in America to study for two years, signaling the disintegration of our adolescent promises. Promises that had become further muddled by resentment and suspicion.

But in that moment, it had felt so natural—like showering after a workout or dressing for the day. So I didn't protest, even though the band laid heavy on a wound that hadn't quite healed. It had felt strange to have a ring on that finger from a man who wasn't Renaldo.

Sliding an olive off the cocktail stick, I pop it into my mouth and chew slowly.

"Jiu-jitsu classes are getting intense," I explain smoothly. "I didn't see you in there." I nod towards the poker room.

He eyes me with frustration before ordering a Jameson on the rocks from the bartender.

"Then you were too focused," he says. "On winning."

I take a long sip of my drink, the pungency of olives and alcohol saturating my mouth.

"How'd you do?" I ask.

"Not even close to as impressively as you."

He shakes his head, as if we've just finished a friendly game on my balcony.

The bartender slides a tumbler towards him, brimming with brown liquor. I press Max Bet and hold two queens.

"You know what they say about losing propositions," I say.

I land a full house, and suck on my cigarette.

Diego shakes his head. "Get out before you get killed."

I tilt up my chin to exhale away from his broad torso, moving in closer as he leans an elbow on the bar. The current between us surges. He swirls the ice in his glass before downing most of his whiskey.

"Unless the risk is worth the reward," he says, placing the near-empty glass on the bar. "Like winning a hundred-fifty-grand pot…on a bluff."

He stares at the cut over my brow. "Jiu-jitsu?"

I gulp down more alcohol, watching his jaw flex from youth and an overabundance of testosterone.

"Are you looking for pointers?" I ask.

One of his large well-manicured hands takes the cigarette from between my fingers. He inhales a final drag slowly before putting out the stub, glancing again at my empty ring finger.

"I want to apologize," he says.

When the call came in, he accused my stepfather of purposely scheming to break up our trip. Worse, he claimed that my working for the man was the reason my mother had landed in the hospital.

I finish my drink and push it away. It's all I can think to do, to calm my nerves. I stand from my chair. In my heels, we're nearly at eye level.

"My mother is out of the hospital," I say. "Thank you." I place a fifty on the bar and press the Cash Out button. "But it doesn't change anything between us."

I slip the paper worth a couple hundred extra now into my clutch and sidle up next to him.

"So fucking hot, aren't you?" My bare shoulder brushes against his jacket, and my cheek flushes as it inches towards his. "But let me be clear." My lips brush his ear. "I'm not interested."

I let that sink in before pouting like I'm about to blow him a kiss and then strutting away, knowing his eyes are still on me.

"Hey," he calls out, but I don't bother turning around.

Diego and I…we're better off as friends. I shouldn't have given him false hope, again.

But he's keeping pace. "Hey," he says, firmly grabbing my arm.

My fist whips up and I nearly clock him.

Reflex.

He lets go and puts some distance between us.

"I know you like to play rough, Victoria." He pauses. "But I also know you're trying to kill my uncle."

I grind to a halt. My heart thumps loudly in my chest.

"Interested now?" Diego places his hand back on my arm and walks me toward a set of elevators.

TWO

The gold-mirrored doors close. We both take out our key cards.

"We can talk in your room, or mine," Diego offers.

I don't rescind my card, so he gestures for me to insert it in the slot.

I punch in the fifty-third floor.

The truth is, I've always been interested in Diego Herrera. The youngest of three sons to Santiago Herrera, he was my schoolmate starting in fifth grade, when my mother and I fled to Mexico after my father's murder in South Africa. My family had employed over a thousand people at our textile company, but that hadn't mattered in a city like Johannesburg during that time of political upheaval. We were white Europeans and a segment of the population hated us solely for that.

Diego was the only one at the private school for international students where I was enrolled who was truly interested in getting to know me. In summer, we spent days on end together, reveling in the awkward ways that we were growing up. And he always defended me—against the boys who teased me for my tall height and big limbs, and the girls who excluded me over my South African accent, my clumsy Spanish, and the line of freckles over my cheeks and nose.

Diego was my friend long before he was my lover.

With a click, the door to my suite latches shut, and the rules of our engagement change from cautiously polite to dangerously familiar. His hand massages the tension in my neck, sending shivers down my spine to my lower back where his hand trails. I yearn for him to tug down my zipper to the same spot, but I know that's not what he's here for right now.

Diego Herrera is first and foremost a loyalist.

The Herreras have long controlled the largest mining corporation in Mexico, with rights to nearly eighty percent of all the gold, silver, and copper in the nation. They are old, well-respected money who foster several high-profile charities.

Diego has always wanted nothing more than to swim in academia and then follow in his family's footsteps. But the stability of their business has been jeopardized over the last few years. Precious metals are losing value in the marketplace as people increasingly invest in technology. And tensions have again mounted between the Herreras and my adoptive family, the Morenos, over several transport routes that have become more heavily used for narcotics than natural resources.

The Morenos have as large a monopoly over transport as the Herreras have over mining. Drugs have always been part of the compromise to thwart bloodshed, but that compromise is being tested. The Herreras have been losing shipments because—they've accused—the Morenos are being paid off by hijackers from one or more cartels. The Morenos assert that it's an inside job.

"Your mother's opiates are coming from José Herrera's distribution network."

My pulse raced when I first heard those words from my stepfather, Vicente. There'd been talk, but a name had never been associated with what had become the Morenos' new drug-trafficking problem, until now. Vicente was certain that Diego's uncle was being compensated handsomely to push through drugs on the Morenos' transport routes. A new type of opiate, to be exact, and in amounts that were causing officials at various government levels to start digging. That was bad for everyone's business.

"You should sit," I say, breaking the silence.

Diego's fingers clench into fists as he moves away from me and plops into a chair next to a circular table.

"What went wrong?" His inquisition begins as he tries to rub the tired off his face. "You had José cornered, alone, in a strip club. His guard was down. He didn't even recognize you at first. So…" he challenges, "why couldn't you kill my uncle?"

I walk toward him but stop short at a chest of drawers.

"I didn't expect anyone to walk into the private back room," I explain honestly. "It was a busy night, and the room was cramped—barely enough space for a dance. But I got close enough. I could've slit his throat with the dagger in my boot." I pull the pack of Pall Malls from my clutch. "But then a girl opened the flimsy door and let in just enough light." I place a cigarette between my lips. "He probably thought he was getting a two-for-one deal—until she started arguing with me and I pushed her."

The mirror over the dresser draws attention back to the cut above my eye and then to Diego shifting to take off his jacket. His white dress shirt tugs against his muscular frame.

"The syringe filled with snake venom dropped out of my cuff," I finish, lighting up my cigarette. "The opportunity was blown."

I don't mention the part about my killing one of José's men in the bathroom, or about José dragging me and the girl out of the club. He caught me off guard with a fist of rings across my brow and then executed the girl swiftly when I wouldn't tell him anything he wanted to hear. When he realized he'd been played by a Moreno, he slammed me to the ground, murmured something obscene about my outfit, and then…both of us saw cop cars in the distance. It was time to leave.

"Nothing happened between us," I assure Diego, slipping out of one stiletto heel followed by the other.

Getting José to believe I was a stripper had been easy. José getting to my knife and gun before I could use either was… unexpected.

I strut towards Diego. Leaning over him, I rub my thumb across his mouth before placing the cigarette between his lips. He untucks my hair from its bun letting it cascade past my shoulders.

I shake out my locks. "Anything else you want to *talk* about?"

THREE

His wrists are bound above his head with the bow tie he wore earlier. My nipples hover over his mouth.

"Where were you tonight, all dressed up?" I demand.

A low moan escapes his lips as Diego lifts his head and tries to catch a piece of succulence between his teeth. But I've already pulled away. He growls in frustration.

"The Herreras threw our yearly casino night charity gala at Rancho Espadas," he explains. "You must have known."

Of course I knew. I knew more than the Herreras wanted me to know. I knew every step they were plotting. I'd learned enough about this world my mother married into to know that as close as I was to the inside, I needed to always have a source who was closer.

I sit up and tug forcefully on the coarse, dark hair of his solid chest. He bites his lower lip, revealing one slightly crooked tooth in an otherwise perfect mouth. I like that he has flaws even though he's been bred not to.

"I knew that party was the last place I should be tonight," I say. "There's a hit out on me." My gaze locks into his. "And they sent you."

His eyelids lower and he exhales sharply. Because once again we're in a compromising situation.

I swivel around to face his magnificent cock.

Two fistfuls of hard delight. A perfect distraction.

I drag my breasts down his torso towards it, my ass tilting up to give him a view that blows away everything on The Strip. His abdomen flexes as my mouth reaches his cock and laps up the pre-cum dripping from the tip.

"I'm not going to kill you, Victoria." His voice is husky.

"There's a weapon in every corner of this suite at my disposal," I say. "Of course you're not going to kill me."

I wrap my lips around his eight-inch steel. *Goddamn, that feels good in my mouth.*

"Ay…dios mío…dame esa panocha," he demands, landing his bound hands on my ass, hard.

The sting makes me hot. His wet tongue reaching my pussy makes me hotter. And the relief…it's like gliding into a pool on a scorching summer day. My mouth relaxes, briefly forgetting the task at hand as he wicks around my folds, sucking on that nub as I inch into position and rock my hips back and forth. I could grind on his face all night.

His hands ply my ass as his thick shaft engorges my mouth, nearly gagging me. But all I can focus on is the growing pressure at my slit. His thumb teases my folds and then moves up that delicate skin to that even-more-delicate opening, popping in just a little. But it's enough for my body to buck as an orgasm ripples through my core. He drives his thumb deeper, electrifying the peak…

With the Vegas lights twinkling in the early morning sky, I collapse onto him, mouth still full of his cock, feeling like I've conquered something. At least in this moment.

I don't come for just every man. In fact, I've only given into one other lover like this. Control is a wicked bitch, but it's as much part of me as it is my dance with Diego since the first time we gave into the heat between us. I rotate my tongue around his shaft, wanting to give him that same amount of pleasure…

"No. Te quiero estar dentro de ti."

Diego likes to speak Spanish when we fuck, and I like to disobey him—sucking harder, swirling faster, and squeezing his sack.

I also like savoring his juices when they explode in my mouth. That massive load. I can't swallow it fast enough—like a satisfying dinner you've just hunted and killed. And then I have to get him hard again, because I need him hard again. I want him inside of me as much as I want to bite into that fresh kill. Not all men can get hard again. Diego always does.

"Dije que no, Victoria," he protests, smacking my ass again with both his palms, lunging me forward.

I roll to my side. "My suite, my rules."

"Fuck your rules." He strains up, his bound hands now in his lap, sweat on his brow. He's not getting out of that constrictor knot anytime soon.

"Untie me," he says.

I slide out of bed and reach for the leather whip I've put under my mattress for protection, my heart beating loudly, swollen knuckles scraping against the box spring. I clutch the rawhide and pull it out, letting the long coil drop to my side. I smack it against the bed and my breathing hastens.

"I'll untie you when I'm ready." My pussy clenches.

His secured hands stroke slowly up and down his hardness, his eyes fixed on mine.

"You have a weapon in every corner," he says, "but we have a man at every casino exit. I'm the only one who can get you out of here alive."

I pounce onto the bed, knocking him back. My black crop stretches tight across his neck. It wouldn't take much pressure to cut off his air… My thighs spread across him and my full breasts heave against his chest. His thick rod is at my wet opening.

I rotate around the tip of his hardness, pulling the rope until he gasps, which makes me gasp, too. The cocktail of fear and excitement creates a perfect aphrodisiac. Slowly, I drag the rope across his neck, feeling the heat from outside seep through the concrete as quickly as the heat seeping between the complicated layers of our relationship.

He coughs to get more air. The whirl of air conditioning finally turns on again in the room.

I can't do it.

The rope drops off the edge of the bed.

Inching down, gripping tight, every rational thought is replaced with something carnal. The instinct that draws two animals together in the most perilous parts of the wilderness. The fit is so tight, but I keep opening and consuming him until I reach the base and then I drop my head to absorb his pheromones. His scent is like a thick sap of salted caramel.

I grind down on him, getting the angle just right. He thrusts up every time I bear down and the pressure builds again, my body burning for a release. I run one hand along his firm torso as it flexes in rhythm to my every craving. My other hand grabs the bow tie, using it as leverage to grind my clit harder, milking his cock for everything I need until I'm coming, lost in a spasm of vulnerable delight.

My body is spent. I want to feel him release inside of me. I want to collapse on top of him. I want to keep fucking like two animals trying to survive a wilderness that is both beautiful and vicious. Our chests heave in a unison that signals it's not over, and he starts pumping into me…

Except I'm not just an animal. I turn my head towards the end table, lean over, and grab his cell phone.

"Call them off." I shove the phone into his palms. "All of them. Tell them I'm not here. That they made a mistake."

Still pumping into me, he stares at me with widened eyes. "Don't be fucking crazy. Let me walk you out of here and make everyone believe you've disappeared. At least for a little while."

He's hitting that spot. That warm and sensitive spot that makes me second-guess every decision and every goal I've ever made or had. That makes me want to curl up and be swept away and taken care of, even though I've never wanted that to be part of my long-term plan—because I've seen everything my mother has gained and lost by being…taken care of.

Diego searches my face for a place to reason. "What I'm offering…they're going to catch up to you eventually. And before you catch up to my uncle again. He's the second-in-line to a multinational business. You killed one of his men last night. You almost killed *him*. You think no one noticed? This would give us…a chance," he pleads.

Although he doesn't say it, it's the same proposal he made on our trip, except without the ring.

I freeze. I'd be lying if I said I wasn't tempted. I've always been tempted. He'll never know how many times I ran my finger around the circumference of that diamond band on the nightstand before I drove off, deciding on a different destiny. I knew the moment I stepped in the old Peugeot that Diego's ring would forever be imprinted on my finger.

But…

"I can't."

My response makes him choke on whatever he was about to say and roar in frustration. He's not the type of man to accept defeat.

His fingers fumble on the phone screen. Awkwardly he holds it against his ear, spitting in Spanish as he does what I've asked him to do.

He throws the phone and then locks his forearms around my neck, pulling me closer to him. His cock is still stiff, and it throbs inside of me, reminding me of why we're even in this position.

Cursing, his lips find mine, biting, absorbing, demanding. And I reciprocate. I have never been unwilling. Our tongues tangle as our bodies rock in unison again.

Sweat trickles down my lower back as I sit up on him. Facing the lights of Sin City, I arch back and grab his full balls, my pussy so sensitive it wouldn't take much to come again. But, no. This time, I want it to be all about him. I ride him—slowly at first, listening to his groans, timing his exhales, reading his signals, and then speeding up, just a little, just what's necessary for him to tell me he's coming. *God, yes, he's coming.* I ride his wave with as much delight as my own.

Utterly satisfied, I collapse on top of him.

A siren wails down the boulevard.

The yellow crest of the sun peeks over the desert dunes.

My fingers walk up his skin and untie the knot around his wrists. His arms slowly drop to his sides.

"I'm worried about you, Victoria." His hands glide across my damp skin.

"You've always worried."

When I dropped out of Uni just a year in, to work for a taqueria in a rough part of town, he warned me I was headed in a reckless direction, forever damning my fate. But I didn't care that he might be right. I had read all the higher education textbooks I was interested in, gotten my essay on the legalization of drugs in a socialist democracy published in *La Opinion,* and had learned how to hunt, fly airplanes, and shoot from my stepfather. A couple of Vicente's guys had even taught me how to build explosives in five different ways. I wanted to forge my own path.

"You're getting in too deep," he admonishes me now, an artery in his neck throbbing. "I don't want to lose you." He presses his lips against my forehead. "You're working for the wrong side."

I could debate with him, but I know that in this world there *is* no right or wrong. It's just a game of advantages.

"I don't want to be locked away," I say, needing him to understand that it's not personal.

His chest rises in frustration. "You'd rather be locked in to peddling arms for the Sinaloas?"

I roll off of him and scold myself for giving in to my weakness. I have no way out of the casino without Diego's help, and he wants to know too much. Maybe to protect me, or maybe to assist his uncle in the shady dealings that are coming to light.

Besides, Vicente only wants a specific type of AK47 because the transport routes are becoming more dangerous for his men, so he needs protection. The short-barrel modification designed for guerilla warfare can't be traced.

"Worry about the shit your own family's peddling," I retaliate.

I open a drawer for a fresh pack of cigarettes and slowly peel back the cellophane.

Diego's body glistens as the heat from outside again seeps through the concrete because the air conditioning has gone off for a while.

"My uncle is not going to be easy."

Still poised at the drawer, I gaze back at him steadily, my fingers dancing over the 9mm hollow-points shoved under a stack of clothes. "I know."

FOUR

My thumb is stained with ink from the newspaper I'm clasping. *The News* is the only English-language daily printed in Mexico City, now on its third resurrection—much like the city itself. I hold my thumb to my mouth and wet it, and then rub it against my well-worn dark-jean skirt. My eyes roam from the page.

The patio at El Pendulo is crammed with people. Inside is just as busy. It's a warm June day, and everyone seems to be caught up in the euphoria of weekend consumerism. They're leaned back, chatting away and laughing as they get hopped up on caffeine and sugar before venturing back out into this trendy part of the city to spend more money in niche, over-priced boutiques feeding off the summer frenzy.

My eyes wander back to the headlines.

New OxyContin Market in the Hands of Criminals and Addicts.

And below that.

City Marks Anniversary of Renaldo Garcia's Death with Candlelight Vigil.

I put down the paper.

My stomach churns as my hand unsteadily picks up the dainty white porcelain filled with a double-shot of espresso. Thick, like sludge. Bitter, like my thoughts.

As I place my lips against the cup, I tilt down my chin to look over my aviators at the woman directly across the café. She's older, but at least a decade younger than my mother. Overdressed for the temperature in leather with fur trimmings, she obviously wants to show off her wealth.

She's a new friend, my mother says, but I don't trust anyone who suddenly sidles up to my mom without a clear connection, like a mutual friend or hobby. This woman came out of nowhere. Met my mother shopping and now wants to meet for lunch or dinner once a week.

It happened shortly after my mom was released from the hospital, proclaiming she was done with the pills. I wanted to get her into rehab—somewhere far away—but she insisted that meeting with her therapist and doctor would be enough…and that she needed some semblance of normal life to get through "this." I told her she was wrong.

My mother, for all her marital obligations, is lonely. An easy target. And this woman, not a staple of Mexico City's high society, is a little too comfortable in this part of town that caters to people who have so much money they can be led to unsavory ends.

The harness around my shoulder is tight and the grip of my Glock pinches the skin under my armpit. I bite into the cookie accompanying my espresso and look back at the paper. At another headline.

Case Remains Open on National Football Team Tragedy.

The picture below it is familiar. Renaldo is on the green lawn of the Estadio Azteca kicking a soccer ball. The muscles in his legs protrude in mid-action as his face contorts in concentration. Sweat glues his shirt to his torso.

He was in his prime.

The sugar on my tongue nauseates me. I try to swallow it and dry heave. I drop the cookie and cover my mouth.

My phone rings and I withdraw it from my purse.

Diego Herrera.

My index finger hesitates and then finally swipes right. Now my stomach churns for a new reason.

It's been three weeks since Las Vegas. I left before he awoke from our tryst and we haven't contacted each other since. That was the right thing to do. I didn't want to leave a trace in Vegas, much less a trace that Diego and I had crossed paths.

"Hey," I answer coolly.

"¿Qué haces, Victoria?" The rumble of his deep voice replaces my nausea with a flutter of anxiety.

"Shopping," I lie.

"Good," he says firmly. "That sounds much better than sitting at a café worrying about the headlines."

Asshole. He's stalking me today of all days, knowing the significance.

My fingers swiftly flip the newspaper page as I scan the cramped patio for any sign of him.

"Are you also....*shopping*?" I ask.

"No," he says, letting out a deep sigh. "That would be a cruel coincidence. Like so many others between us."

Of course. I'm not the only one with eyes all over Mexico City.

My gaze lands back on the paper. A photo of the whole soccer team imprints like a negative the harder I squeeze my eyes. The first time Diego and I fucked, I was mourning the loss of my first lover—Renaldo Garcia.

Renaldo was Central Defender and Captain of Mexico's national football team. We met at a boisterous World Cup event in South Africa after Mexico beat out Spain. The kind of event that starts late in the evening and doesn't end until the sun comes up, and that you can only get into if you're beautiful, rich, or powerful. It was the first time I'd been back to Johannesburg since my father's murder, and also the first time I could enjoy the mayhem as an adult.

It didn't take long for Renaldo to notice me. He was wild and outspoken in that way you have to be when you come from nothing, and he had the kind of seniority and talent that easily ascended him to team captain.

His tenacity was unapologetic, even if some called it obnoxious and pushy. We were similar in that way, which is what made us butt heads like rams. But that only stoked the fire. He would take control and make decisions like they were never wrong, and I would call him a cocky chauvinist, battling and questioning him at every step until we ended up naked in the kitchen or bedroom, turning our fury into the kind of newfound fervor you have only when you've just transitioned from virgin to sexually empowered woman at the hands of a confident and experienced man.

Our relationship was as contentious in the gossip rags as it was privately. The headlines swung from *Hot Couple of the Year* to our twelve-year age gap and the inevitability of Renaldo going back to his bachelor ways. Six months into our whirling affair, to put the rumors of his intentions with me to rest, Renaldo proclaimed that we were getting married. It's one of the few things I didn't contest, because I wanted it as much as he did.

We were planning a summer wedding, with my mother's blessing. Marriage was going to reign me in and give me some responsibility and purpose in life, she said. Vicente, too, gave a supportive nod.

But then Renaldo's boat blew up.

"Almost as cruel of a coincidence as my uncle ending up at the same café as you," Diego interrupts my reverie, "after....*shopping*."

I'm startled back to reality. This time I scan for the Herrera who's been unexpectedly forcing my hand since my return from Vegas. It's become clear he wants to toy with me more than he wants me dead. That because I failed once, he assumes I'll fail again. But his lax approach has allowed me to figure out the details of his operation. Like his facility being on the outskirts of Mexico City, about an hour away. And his cheap opiate supplies coming from somewhere in Barbados.

Finally, I spot him...joining the woman I've been watching for nearly half an hour.

Why am I not surprised?

He's dressed almost as grandiose as she is, in a three-piece pin-striped suit with a fedora to match. Not like a scumbag who frequents shady strip clubs and cuts cheap opiate supplies with heroin.

As they kiss on the cheek, their body language signals familiarity. José's reputation as a womanizing piece of shit precedes him, but I don't care about that. I care about this "friend" of my mother being tied to a man who knows how to make a powerful concoction at a persuasive street price.

I turn away from the couple towards the glaring sun, adjusting my sunglasses. "Let me call you later."

Diego clears his throat loudly. "Let me tell you about the two men dressed in white shirts and light jeans at your six o'clock."

My fingers roll an edge of the newspaper back and forth before glancing in that direction. *All* of José's thugs appear to be in the café. They must have shown up right before José.

"Maybe I should introduce myself."

"This is not a joke, *mi amor*."

My heart races. It's something about the way he says those words. *Mi amor...* Different from the way Renaldo used to say them. I turn back to the couple.

Except they're gone. I scramble to grab my purse, keys, and jacket, doing a final visual sweep of the café. "I have to go."

"Victoria!" Diego yells through my phone as it slips from between my ear and shoulder. I barely save it from hitting the ground as I make my way through tightly spaced tables and chairs.

Turning back, I see two men in white shirts tracing my footsteps. A small child steps in front of me. I shove him and get an earful from the mother, but the two men are nearing.

Pushing past the crowd at the host stand, I burst through the front door and duck behind a group of girls milling around the valet station. Seeing me, they whisper like… they've just been reading the same paper I have.

I see José and the woman talking as two separate cars arrive. José hands her a slip of paper before stepping into a black Land Rover and driving away. The woman scans the paper and starts texting as she heads to the driver's side of the white Renault pulled up for her.

Grasping the leather of my shoulder harness, I jog a few steps so I can view the license plate.

A finger taps me on the shoulder.

"Señorita, señorita." The squat waiter is out of breath and waving a bill.

As I pull out my wallet and thumb through pesos, I see the two white-shirts approach the valet stand and point towards me, arguing with a man who looks to be the manager. I mouth to the waiter that I'm sorry, indicating that I've been fleeing those two men and that they appear to have guns.

I hand the now wide-eyed staffer more than enough to cover my tab.

Squatting down behind a car that's just been dropped off, I watch the woman step into her Renault. José's thugs are now surrounded by security.

I shuffle toward the rear of the vehicle, pop open the back door, and jump in. The eyes of the valet driver meet mine in the rearview mirror. Crouched on the floor of the backseat, I wave him forward with a pleading look.

Once we're away from the commotion I've created at the valet stand, he peers at me again in the rearview mirror and smiles.

"Diego es mi amigo," he says.

Smiling back, I slide up onto the expensive leather.

"My car is parked down the street, *por favor*," I say, handing him more than enough pesos to cover the inconvenience. But he waves away my money.

He pulls up to my black Challenger, and I don't question how he knows the make and model of my vehicle.

"Gracias, amigo," I say, stepping out of the sedan.

My fingers hit the unlock button on my remote. Doing a three-sixty, I check for any potential pursuers before climbing into the driver's seat and locking my doors. Fumbling in my purse for my phone, I pull out the newspaper again instead, opened to one of the articles I was reading.

Two small pop-out pictures catch my attention. One is of me and Renaldo, the other, Renaldo with an ex-girlfriend. The caffeine swirls through my veins, spiking my body temperature.

Some bitch always has to chime in with her opinion about Renaldo's death, I fume. *And our relationship.*

It's reader bait. Because I will never talk about the day Renaldo's boat blew up.

I slam the paper shut, jam my key into the ignition, and scream out of the alley in reverse.

Renaldo's boat blew up into so many tiny pieces, nothing and no one could be identified by much more than the itinerary that placed them there. He'd gone on a sailing trip with five of his closest teammates in between the regular season tournaments—something they'd been doing for years. But this time they never made it back.

The country mourned six of its top players and speculations ran rampant, even though no one dared declare it anything but an accident. An "undetected fuel leak." I had my own theory.

My eyes land on the screen of my phone. Two missed calls from Diego and several texts.

Call me.

My fingers grip the steering wheel.

I need to find the Renault first.

FIVE

The white Renault pulls out of the warehouse owned by a shell company I've traced to Diego's uncle. I've followed Teresa Guzmán to the heavily-guarded facility four times since spotting her with José at the café.

Hidden from casual observers, the warehouse sits in a valley below the peaks of the Mexican high desert. With no other structures for miles, there's no reason for anyone to be out here without specific cause.

Since that day at the café, I've been as preoccupied with Teresa as with José. After attending a high-profile event, she was recently documented in astounding detail in Mexico City's social pages, from which I learned that from "humble beginnings in the Sonora province," she came to Mexico City a year ago under the guise of a pharmacologist. But her obvious ties to José Herrera have made it clear to me that Teresa is peddling high-strength opiates to people who can't—or are too ashamed to—ask their doctor for prescriptions to heal an emotional pain they can't explain.

People like my mother.

I toss my bottle of water onto my empty passenger seat and start my engine. I carefully traverse the rocky ledge, keeping an eye on the paved road below.

My mother relapsed. Last week, I discovered her lying unconscious on the bathroom floor, just like a stereotypical addict. She'd exhibited warning signs again—irritability, low energy, hot sweats—which she had continued to blame on menopause as she had for the past two years. But I had connected the dots of this relapse to her "friendship" with Teresa.

Once her body was pumped dry of opiates, I questioned my mother relentlessly. It wasn't Teresa's fault, she assured me—before her there'd been another woman. But, she admitted, Teresa had access to something stronger.

Up ahead is a less obvious entrance to the paved road, but the dirt path is steep. One bad slip of a tire…luckily I am traveling downhill, not up. I shift into third and crank the steering wheel left.

I'm not surprised that my mother got hooked on pills. The thrill of being married to one of the most powerful men in Mexico wore off years ago. Vicente's attention had faded quickly after he got what he wanted. A beautiful woman on an aging bachelor's arm, with a built-in kid so he didn't have to worry about making one.

She'd wanted more.

My mom is vowing to go to rehab this time, which is good. But I know none of this would be happening if my dad were still alive. She had something with him she and Vicente will never have. That's why she was willing to risk her life to be with my father in South Africa during the political turmoil—and now, in an afterlife she is convinced exists.

I tip over an edge that drops me like an elevator down a chute, with a view of the valley that would make anyone queasy from a ninety-degree angle. My palms sweat as I carve downward as slowly as possible, the low hum of RPMs grinding in my eardrums as I make sure not to brake too hard, which could send my vehicle toppling. My breathing hastens as I make a final sharp left onto the paved road.

I pop the Challenger into first, sending it screaming until I've caught up to the white Renault. Not much longer before we reach a more populated area where it will be impossible to make this look like an accident—at least at first. This two-lane road connects to an arterial that leads into the city from the east.

I reach for the sawed-off shotgun lying on the seat next to my water bottle. Perspiration forms on my brow. My right thigh stiffens as I bear down on the accelerator, gaining enough on the Renault that at the next turn I can pop my shotgun out the window and aim for Teresa's rear passenger-side tire. Her car should spin into the guardrail with enough speed—or a purposeful nudge—to fly over the top of it and crash into the valley below.

We reach the turn and I fire…and miss.

As Teresa decelerates to control the sharp curve along the winding pass, my shot hits her fender. *Shit.*

The echoing blast startles her. The Renault swerves but then speeds away, snaking through the bends. Finally, a curve sends her drifting far enough into the oncoming lane for me to get on her passenger side. I ram my gearshift into second so I can focus on the necessary shot.

Seeing me, she begins screaming profanities. My heart pounds loudly and I open my mouth…to pop the pressure in my ears. My left wrist cramps as I pump the gun against the passenger seat before thrusting it out my driver's side window. Her eyes widen.

I take my second shot at her front right tire. This time I don't miss.

As her car spins towards mine, the haze of gunpowder clouds my vision. But only for a moment. I've got more maneuverability…and a singular purpose.

The white Renault skids into a large boulder at the edge of the dusty road. My Challenger screeches to a stop to the right of it.

Transfixed by the mangled metal and shattered glass, I pull the handle of my car door and kick it open wide. Unable to help myself, I step out and walk around the wreck, as if contemplating changing my plan and saving her life even though she has threatened my mother's.

From the driver's side, I study the airbag deployed into Teresa's face. That face that wears too much makeup and those clothes that are too grandeur for a dirty hustler. Her gasps are accompanied by the chemical smell of burning rubber.

I'm not going to lose my mother, too.

I lift my shotgun to the side of Teresa's head, pump it, and without further hesitation, pull the trigger. The passenger side of the Renault explodes in red.

My gaze remains fixed until the vein in her neck stops twitching.

The shotgun handle is imprinted in my skin, but my hand has no tremor—not like after my first kill. I shake out my left arm and do one last pan of the scene. This time my gaze lands on boxes in the Renault's back seat. The small label reads *XYTocetHydro355*. My free fingers reach into my back pocket for my cell phone and I snap a picture. As a murder of crows caw from the trees overhead, flapping their wings to depart, I climb back into the Challenger.

Tossing my weapon back on the passenger seat, I start up the engine and reverse back onto the road. I drive in silence, clutching my phone, until the two-lane road expands to four lanes and more cars appear in front, next to, and behind me.

I can't decide where to go.

Vicente and my mother's house would be too obvious, and I vacated my apartment weeks ago after it was ransacked by José's men in retaliation for Vegas. The tiny studio above the taqueria where I used to work would feel too…empty, right now. Plus, I don't want to throw any suspicion at Hector, the owner. He's a good man who doesn't deserve trouble.

My hands relax around the steering wheel as I scroll to Diego's number.

"Hola," he answers.

His voice is brusque, but a relief. Now that I hear it, I barely know what to say. I go with something banal.

"How are you?"

"Fine. Working."

My throat pinches. Since that day at the café, he's wanted to see me—at his place, a hotel, a vacant apartment his parents own, even an obscure venue. But I've refused. Saying it's too risky. Not so much because people are trying to kill me, but because I have little resistance around Diego.

I question myself daily over the distance I'm putting between us. A distance that just a few months ago felt like it was melting. Even now, as I weave through the busy streets of the city center, I question whether even calling him is giving into a subconscious thought, a reflex, a weakness, or if I'm just using him.

Diego Herrera is a desire I can't quell. But with my pursuit of José and anyone affiliated with his new business becoming an obsession and the ghost of Renaldo fading over time, Diego has become my only connection to a real-world sanity that I feel slipping daily. Disappearing on him again…not returning his calls or texts, brushing him off with excuses… it feels like the worst crime I've committed.

You're going to lose focus on your priorities.

It's my greatest concern every time I contemplate spending time with Diego.

"Working late at Polanco?" I ask, playing with the knobs of the radio. The frequency lands on some grupera-style song. A popular mix of ranchera and rock that probably scaled the charts in the eighties.

"I'm at La Roca de Oro," he responds gruffly.

Odd that Diego is at his parents' ranch. He usually spends Fridays at the Herreras' downtown business headquarters and then stays at his nearby apartment in the upscale neighborhood of Polanco.

"I always liked the ranch," I say.

The small talk is ridiculous. The silence is long. The music on the radio is irritating me. I play with the knobs again and land on some techno music that's popular in the clubs right now.

"My parents are on vacation," he informs. "You should visit again."

His words knot my stomach.

"I don't think that's a good idea."

I shove the shotgun under the front seat as the cityscape dances in front of me.

He curses under his breath. "I think— It's a safe place for you right now."

With his familiar overtone peppering the landscape, I turn off the main road and pull over to gather my thoughts.

I tug at the handle of my glove compartment until it falls open. I grab the pack of Pal Malls inside and flip open the box.

"It might take me some time to get there."

I pull out a cigarette, along with the lighter wedged in the carton.

"Take your time. There's less traffic on the backroads. You know how to get here on the backroads. ¿*Sí?*" His voice is a steady compass in my chaotic mind.

I take a long drag as I reverse my car. "*Sí.*"

Desire is a selfish bitch.

SIX

I pull off the dirt road leading up to the Herreras' ranch and park behind a stable that is unusually abandoned save for the whinny of a few horses. I roll down my window and inhale deeply, nostrils flaring to absorb the smell of dried hay and dewy grass.

Five years. Almost to the day.

The last time I was here was for a party to celebrate the Summer Solstice. The Morenos were always invited and we always attended. Before business took priority over decades of friendship, that is.

I shut the door of my Challenger and sweep the surroundings. Five years…but everything about this place, including the drive, feels like walking down a memory lane of simpler times.

The crunch of my boots on the loose gravel reverberates loudly against the wooden stalls. Usually several ranch hands are milling about, even at sunset. But today, no one appears to greet me or make small talk, or offer to help with me with some physical task.

I make my way across the expansive property to the main house. The Herreras own hectares of land out here.

Out here. The last place on earth I thought I'd end up.

My boots kick up dust, sending it swirling in my path. When I was younger, I came out here all the time. So often, it felt like a second home. The rolling green hills with barren mountain peaks in the distance created a mixed landscape of desert and plains that was peaceful and reflective. It reminded me of our home in South Africa.

I trudge towards the colossal estate as the sun starts to dip below the horizon. The white-washed exterior façade, the rust-colored ceramic roof tiles, and the imported sweeping palm trees give the grounds a Mediterranean texture that is nothing like anything else this far outside Mexico City. Excess by any standards, but not surprising for the Herreras.

I near the familiar wrought-iron gate.

Diego's '71 Plymouth Road Runner is in the circular driveway. A rush of unease flows through my body. Being with Diego…*out here*…

My heart palpitates as my mind races with possible scenarios that maybe this is a trap. Maybe he's changed his mind about me. I shouldn't have called.

No. He wouldn't do that. Not yet.

The hair on the back of my neck tingles as I press my arm against the holster under my arm.

There are three ways to get through this barricade that surrounds the entire house. You can drive in with a Herrera, get on the reception list to have the gate opened, or punch in the code. I've watched Diego punch in the code many times. I memorized it years ago because it's never changed.

My fingers land on the metal numbers of the keypad and then rescind. If this *is* a setup, the front gate is too obvious.

There's a back gate. Diego and I have gone through it enough times, especially in high school, whenever we had to sneak back in after missing curfew.

I slither towards the rear of the property, scanning the grounds like a sniper, keeping an eye out for anything unusual.

The entire property is eerily quiet.

I spot the security box and stalk towards it. As my fingers dance over the pattern I remember, I take in a deep breath. This time the scent penetrating my membranes is from the nearby rose bushes. I glance at the delicate white flowers, stifling a snicker.

Diego insisted on picking some of those for me late one night after far too much mescal. The liquor made him forget how tough the branches were, and thorn-laden.

It's often the beautiful ones that make you bleed.

The lock clicks open and I turn the knob of the steel door to let myself onto the property.

Past the tennis court and pool, I spot the gymnasium. The window drapes are pulled back and I see Diego inside.

His bare torso glistens. Every now and then, he tosses his hair out of his eyes, which are glued to the news on the wall-mounted flat-screen. They're reporting an accident on Highway 57.

I inch my way forward. A close-up of the white Renault flashes across the screen, its former glory now barely discernible.

Fingering the coarse stalk of the palm tree I'm hunkered

behind, I watch an ambulance and police cars flood the TV screen.

Diego picks up a jump rope. His biceps and forearms flex as his meaty legs maneuver over the cord with grace. In school, he was one of those athletes who excelled at everything he tried. Built for strength and mobility, with the stamina of a horse.

He drops the rope and lies back on a bench. He wraps his fingers around the bar, its ends loaded with plates of steel. He frees it from its hinges, pressing up and down, chest puffing, abdomen sucking in…

It makes me want to rub myself until I come.

I did that once. Near the beginning of our love affair, after hooking up at the taqueria. It was one of the few times I spent the night, awakening in his top-floor flat, lavish in size but barren in furnishings, giving it a twinge of youthfulness that I liked. A true bachelor pad. Seeing him exercising in front of the floor-to-ceiling windows, I crept to a spot in the room where I wouldn't disturb him but where he would notice me, leaned back against the wall, and pleasured myself. Coming for him as he crunched his abdomen…the way he's crunching it now.

I saunter out from behind the palm.

I grab a handful of pebbles and throw them at a window. His arms jerk as he looks in my direction.

The door to the gymnasium is open. I tiptoe onto the bare wooden floor, the ceiling's exposed beams creating a musty humidity laced with leather and chalk. Near the entranceway, water runs cyclically over a marble fountain. My fingers create a ripple as I touch the nude male bust.

"It's quiet here tonight," I say.

He replaces the bar. His tattoo of the Mexican flag inside classic Aztec art lines flexes on his shoulder.

"My parents left for Tulum yesterday. The family is meeting there for vacation."

I rest my elbows on the leather backrest of a piece of workout equipment, the cut of my shirt digging into my cleavage.

"Sounds nice."

"Join us," he says like a dare, sitting up. His eyes shift across my body.

"We're not kids anymore," I remind him.

"That's not a bad thing." He reaches for a sports bottle, pops the top, and leans back. The water cascades into his mouth, missing a corner and leaving a slick trail down the edge of his chin and pectoral.

The news reporter is now discussing that the police are now saying the car discovered run off the road was intentional, a murder.

I nod at the television. "How did she get involved with José?" I ask, stepping towards him and placing my boot toe on the base of the bench he's sitting on. "Was she a family friend?"

He closes the cap of the bottle before tossing it to the side.

"I should have known," he sneers. "Isn't it late for you to be gathering *inteligencia,* after the day you've had?"

The bottle rolls away and he lies back under the bar, gripping it like he's ready to get back to his workout and dismiss me.

"Do you know about the facility in Los Cuartos?" I prod,

crossing my arms. "Where your uncle is manufacturing the opiates?"

He grunts and lifts up the weights. All the major arteries bulge under his skin as he starts pressing again.

"What I know," he says, "is that you're being reckless."

I shuffle my feet along either side of the bench, my jean skirt stretching tightly across my thighs, until I'm over his midsection.

"There were photos of you and Teresa at that event," I say.

He hoists the bar back into secure position.

"Did it make you jealous, Victoria? Make you want to kill me, too?"

"No, I—" I relax my arms and tuck strands of hair behind my ear. "Thank you for letting me come here tonight."

His mouth curls as his fingers play with an edge of denim. "No one even knows *I'm* here tonight."

I purposefully lower myself until the polyester of his shorts and the silk of my underwear are the only two things standing in our way.

"It's unusual." I gaze out the windows. "The quiet."

His hands grip my thighs firmly, sending a bolt of electricity through my torso.

"A realtor is coming tomorrow to show the place, so they gave the staff a few days off. They're thinking about selling. They want to be closer to the rest of the family, in the city, maybe build an estate somewhere else. A Saudi has already offered them the kind of money that shouldn't be refused."

I lean forward, my nails trailing down his chest.

"I've always loved it out here," I say. "I hope they don't do it."

His cock stiffens beneath the fabric.

His fingers run up my clothes, grazing at the buttons of my shirt. He pops the top one. I rock forward and backwards over his hard-on. Everything is wet in moments. His fingers trace along the lace of my bra, until they reach the sturdy leather of my holster.

"You carry this everywhere now?" he asks.

I freeze. "I don't want to be caught off guard."

"Take it off," he demands.

I straighten and slowly peel off my jacket.

He shakes his head and thrusts both hands under my armpits. "Grab the bar above you."

I stretch for the curved pull-up bar.

His palm grabs the handle of my Glock and jerks it out of my holster. My mouth opens to protest, but before I can say anything, he checks that the safety is on and then thrusts the barrel downward, hooking the front of my button-up shirt.

Buttons clink on hardwood.

"I said, take it off," he demands again, sliding the gun across the floor.

Hovering over him, I search his dark eyes for the type of candidness we've always shared.

"I saw her walk into your downtown headquarters," I tell him.

His breath is hot on my stomach as he grabs the leather of my holster and unsnaps the strap holding it together. He yanks it over my shoulders.

"Venture capital. Nothing more."

My palms are sweating, but I try to not completely lose my self-control. "For—"

"Shhhhh…" he quiets as his fingers wander backwards, first to my ass and then sliding my underwear to one side to slip between my folds.

I gasp, almost forgetting…

"For what?" I persist.

He removes his fingers abruptly. "A new drug for people with an opioid addiction," he replies impatiently.

He stands. Remnants of a musky cologne penetrate my nostrils like a lucid aphrodisiac.

But something doesn't add up.

"Since when did the Herreras start investing in pharmaceuticals?"

He grabs my chin, running a thumb over my lower lip.

"Since when do I have to go over my family's business details with someone who's refused my ring?"

I step back from him, searching for the right words. "You don't need…*that*, right now."

He winds the leather across my lower back and pulls me into him. "Then maybe you don't need any of *this*, right now, either."

My chest heaves into his. "Fuck you, Diego." I push away from him, but he pulls me in tighter.

"Let go of the bar," he says hoarsely.

I uncurl my fingers and drop my arms.

He walks around me and tugs at my top until it falls.

I look towards my gun, weighing my options. It's not too late to leave.

He unclasps my bra. My breasts fall freely.

The hide of my holster running down my back sends shivers.

Fuck me. I don't want to leave.

"Bend over," he commands.

I do as he says, clutching the sides of the narrow bench as he lifts up my skirt. The holster trails further down until it reaches my wet opening. He gently slaps me with the leather. My clit pulses.

"You're dangerous, *mi amor,*" he says.

"The way you like it," I reply, envisioning his cock entering me.

He gently smacks my ass cheek. "No, the way *you* want it."

The light sting makes me hotter, and I tilt my ass towards him. He wraps the leather around my thighs this time, pulling me to him until I feel the tip of his cock at my opening, pulsing and stretching me.

Panting, I inch backwards, wanting more. His grip tightens around the leather strap as he pulls me into him, our breaths becoming hurried as I completely absorb his cock.

We glide in and out, me opening more for him each time so he can hit my deepest of pleasure spots. He lets go of the leather and drives harder, grasping the back of my hair.

"Quédate conmigo," he whispers in my ear.

As his tongue licks at the irregular orifice, I lose myself in the physical indulgence of the moment and gasp at the additional fullness of his cock. I clench around him, the pressure building…

Continuing to tug my hair, his other hand moves up my stomach to my breast, cupping it and then squeezing my nipple, enough to get my attention. I almost yelp out.

Our rhythm speeds up and he moves his palm over my

clit, urgently flicking his fingers so that we can come together. He's swelling inside of me and I know he's ready to explode.

"Come for me, baby," his voice rasps, as he holds back, waiting for me.

I circle my hips to the motion of his fingers, our excitement intensifying, our grunts louder. I tighten around his rod again, the sweet nectar building until the wave hits a peak I know I'm about to ride.

My mouth widens into a muted cry as I unleash, savoring the release as it unwinds from my hot pussy all the way down to my toenails.

As my orgasm begins to subside, he pounds harder and faster, and I brace for his explosion, which fills me to the tips of every nerve-ending as much as my own did. With his last thrust, he presses firmly into me until he's unloaded every last drop.

"Holy fuck," he says, echoing my own thoughts.

He pulls out, his erection slick with our juices. Legs trembling, we collapse in a heap on a nearby mat.

We're both still panting.

Enveloped in his arms, I feel his fingers gently massage my scalp.

"You should stay here tonight," he offers. "It will be safer."

The blades of the fan above us rotate with a dull whirl. I couldn't will my body to move if I tried.

"You're the ace up my sleeve," I tell him gratefully.

"I won't always be."

My cheek grazes his, and my lips bite at the salty skin of his neck until I reach his mouth. I dive in for another taste.

SEVEN

I turn off the main street into a part of town that is always suspicious of strangers…but that I am no stranger to.

The kids playing stick ball in the street part to let me through just as two men scurry into an alley next to some new construction. Tepito is still a shady area, regardless of efforts to gentrify this old colonial center.

I slowly park the dated Honda Civic I'm driving behind a stripped-down Toyota Celica, in front of the taqueria I used to work at.

I told Diego I needed to get rid of the Challenger. He understood. The next morning, the valet who rescued me at El Pendulo showed up with my replacement vehicle.

The bells in the church across the street ring out six times. The cross hanging from my rearview mirror rocks to their beat double-time. People are gathered, but not the typical weekend devotees. Across from the modest stone church is a shrine to La Santa Muerte.

The Angel of Death.

I pull at the handle of the glove box. It sticks, but finally it flips open and I spot a pack of mashed Pall Malls in there. Tearing open the top, I'm relieved to find two left. I grab one and then pat around the compartment for a lighter until my fingers stroke the familiar hard plastic.

Walking towards the taqueria, I click until a flame appears and puff at the end of the cigarette until it burns.

"¡Dé fuerza a mi familia!" a woman hollers, clutching the hand of a small child and wiping back tears with a trembling hand. A cigarette falls from between her fingers, compelling me to check the status of mine.

Resting my hand on the gate to the taqueria's small patio, I watch as a nearby couple holding a gift box helps the woman towards the grinning skeleton draped in a white wedding gown, displayed in a large glass enclosure. Santa Muerte will protect those no one else will in their darkest hour. That is the enduring folklore passed down from the pre-Columbian era of Mexico. The woman reaches her hand towards the macabre matron.

I push open the gate and head for one of the weathered tables. The old taqueria looks the same as ever with its colorful chipped paint and traditional murals on the walls. Hector calls out to me by name before strolling over to give me a hug. He verifies my usual order, carne asada tacos and a Modelo, and I nod. He pulls out a chair and guides me to sit. Hector knows when I need to just sit.

Moments later, I put out my half-smoked cigarette in an ashtray and tip back the bottle of Modelo against my lips. My boot taps against the dusty wooden floor, the dirt beneath my fingernails making it look like I've been tilling fields. The woman at the shrine is now wailing uncontrollably.

Working here, I've seen it all. People mocking, praying, stealing, singing, showering gifts, getting shit-faced, and passing out around that fancy relic that the Catholic Church deems a means for drug dealers to escape hell.

Stop thinking about false prophets and trim your nails before people start wondering what kind of work you're really doing, I chide myself.

A loud cheer emanates from the small group of men sitting at the bar. I glance up at the football playing on the television. Even though it's an exhibition game, Mexico just scored and the sportscasters are heralding the team's new captain.

Teeth grinding, I look away and pick at the label of my beer.

My phone rings. I shouldn't but…I reach into my purse. It's Diego. I swipe at the red X on the screen.

Last night I stayed like he wanted me to, bathed in the crest of the moon as he tightened his palm around my neck and pressed his hardness against the small of my back, my pussy quivering like a bird unable to fly away quickly enough from a storm. But I can't pick up the phone right now.

On the television, the face of Mexico's new captain is magnified and the men surrounding the bar compare him to the captain that came before him, Renaldo Garcia.

My tacos arrive and Hector puts a firm hand on my shoulder. He asks if I'm alright, and I nod mutely because if I open my mouth I may break apart and scream, much like the woman at the shrine. I glance once more at the monitor over the bar. The face of Mexico's new captain is gone. Hector releases my shoulder and walks away.

I grab a piece of carne from the corn tortilla and place it on my tongue, chewing the shredded meat until it's void of all flavor and tastes like nothing more than death. Then I take another gulp of *cerveza* and glance at my phone. Diego wants to know that I've made it back to somewhere safe.

I look back at the television, now alive with football highlights from the previous season.

It was Diego's idea to have dinner together two days after Renaldo left for the boat trip that ended up being his last. Diego was upset about my engagement, and insistent that I reconsider Renaldo's proposal. Diego had never even considered that while he was studying in America, I'd start a relationship with another man. I hadn't planned on it, either. It was Vicente's idea for my mother and me to take a vacation to South Africa.

When I told Diego I had no intention of breaking things off, he became unusually desperate. Pleading with words I'd never heard in his vocabulary. Words that made me feel so guilty that the only way I could think to make him stop was to hurt him…

I told him I loved Renaldo like I would never love another man, which is why I had given myself to him.

Diego's silence turned to disgust.

We had talked about saving ourselves. But that felt like another time in another world. Could he really have thought that after being away for two years…? He called me a *puta* before wishing me well—a sentiment that didn't even scrape the surface of authentic.

But then Renaldo's boat blew up. I spent months paralyzed with grief, unable to eat, sleep, or talk. My mother begged me to do something—therapy, work, a vacation—but I couldn't imagine going back to anything I knew prior to Renaldo. Instead, I took up Vicente on his offer to fly banknotes out of an airport in Puebla, a couple hours south of town.

I was shocked Vicente even offered me the job. He's never hidden his sexism. Except for the social need to have a woman on his arm, he surrounds himself with men. He's quiet and reclusive, the complete opposite of my father in many ways.

Plus, Vicente and I didn't always get along—until I demanded he take me hunting with him. So his job offer seemed like an olive branch. And a belief in my abilities, which he'd never communicated before. My mother didn't approve, but Vicente assured her nothing would happen to me and that I'd likely grow out of it fast and find another husband.

The job suited me. I honed my pilot skills and didn't have to talk to much of anyone outside of Moreno's men, who loaded and unloaded the small planes with things I never questioned. I did this for damn near a solid year, rarely returning home.

It was a lazy summer weekend, much like this one, when Diego found me swimming in beer and lapping up tacos in this old taqueria.

A guy about my age walks up to my table. I've never seen him before, but I've definitely seen his type. Baggy pants, oversized t-shirt, ill-fitting baseball cap…a low-level player trying to make a mark. I wonder if he's one of José's men.

He issues a few lame come-ons, blatantly ignoring my attempts to wave him off. So I swallow the bite of dinner I've been contemplating on and politely explain to him that he needs to leave me alone. My response is not to his liking and he leans in too close for my comfort. The skin surrounding the gun under my arm sweats as I consider shooting this kid point-blank, right in front of everyone. But I don't want to do that to Hector. Hector's been good to me.

The homeboy rests a hand on my arm as his other reaches for…a piece near his abdomen.

He *is* one of José's men.

The scream I wanted to unleash earlier releases in the form of an uppercut to his jaw, my body rising to gain maximum leverage. It's enough of a surprise that he fumbles in his retrieval of what looks to be a .38 Special.

My boot connects with his thigh as Hector appears beside me, telling me to stand back. The heads of a few employees pop out from the kitchen. No one is going to pull a weapon now. Hector has the protection of this neighborhood.

As Hector escorts the guy well down the street, the thug spouts out loud accusations about my being a killer. I see the men at the bar looking at me much the same way those women at the valet stand did at the café…like they know too much about me.

My airway passages constrict. Gasping for breath, I run into the bathroom, slam the door, and turn the lock.

I would never have contacted Diego so soon after Renaldo's death of my own volition. I wanted to be alone.

But he sat down uninvited and didn't waste time expressing his concerns over my prolonged silence. I was ambivalent to his presence until he told me he'd found out that his parents had deliberately sent him to Uni in America to separate us. That they had manipulated our destiny as much as I had done so by insisting on marrying Renaldo instead of committing to our fate.

How dare he malign Renaldo? I spat in his face and accused him of having a hand in destroying my future.

He smacked me. Hard enough for me to know how deeply I'd offended him. I told him that made him all the more suspicious.

He downed the rest of my *cerveza* and began shoveling in the food that had been set before me. Spicy carne dripped onto his light green t-shirt and sweat stained his armpits as he chewed each bite intently. As intently as he was trying to convince me I was wrong.

The carne was hot. Hot, like the hell I told him I'd make sure he'd burn in if I ever found out he or his family had anything to do with Renaldo's death.

He ordered two more Modelos as the sun descended and the band started up inside the taqueria. He grabbed ahold of my hand. I tried to wriggle free. He tightened his grip and swung me off my chair, pressing my body against his as I tried to protest. But his physicality overpowered me, reminding me of the sexuality Renaldo had awakened in me a year earlier. The sexuality I was now mourning as much as the man.

At first I felt guilty for allowing my hatred and suspicions to drown in the commanding muscles of Diego's torso. Muscles that had become larger and more defined since our attraction first ignited years ago. But as he buried his face in my hair and we got lost in the bustle and sharp scents of that packed dance floor, I knew this was part of me taking care of myself.

My breasts rubbed against his rib cage as his hands wandered down my ass and we grinded slowly against each other as though our clothes weren't part of the equation. As though we were finishing what we'd started back in high school. A fiery make-out session in his car laden with words of unconditional love, which usually leads to everything else except…that we decided to save ourselves for something bigger.

It had seemed so simple at the time. We could never have imagined how our world would be torn apart.

That night on the dance floor, my mouth dove into Diego's as tears trickled down my face, my fingers clambering to replace everything I'd lost, even though I knew I'd never replace Renaldo. I would only find something different.

But I needed to find something. Renaldo wasn't coming back. I needed something—someone—to fill the void…and to quiet the heat between my thighs. I hated myself for the thought as my fingers gripped Diego's neck and I felt his growing hardness pinned against my thigh, but it only made me wetter.

We fucked in this same cramped bathroom of the taqueria. With its piss stains on the floor, its ripped-off toilet seat in the corner, and its sink severing off a wall filled with love notes and promises of a good time.

Fists pounding against the door made me want to pop a cap into whoever was on the other side. But Diego stopped my hand as it moved down my calf toward my Glock. And as soon as he entered me, I lost track of all reality. That thick cock filled me like a violent storm that hits without warning. I knew right then it would break my resistance. I would make mistakes because of the night we spent fucking in his penthouse after he called his car to pick us up from the taqueria.

I turn on the tap of a newly installed sink and splash my face with water. The walls have been painted, the floors cleaned up with new tile, and…I can breathe again.

As I open the door, I can hear the band warming up for their evening performance. My table has been pushed to make space for the dance floor, and a fresh beer awaits me on the bar. But I can't risk it.

I need to get out of here.

I salute Hector as I pass him, checking the exits for anyone who looks to be one of José's men. My steps become more hurried as I cross the threshold of the taqueria and head toward a staircase hidden by the natural landscape, which leads up to the small studio Hector has been letting me stay in. I need to shower and then sleep for a few hours.

My phone buzzes. Pausing at a planter box, I flick off a fly that's landed on a leaf before reaching into my back pocket.

XBWX3 departing for Barbados tomorrow at 5GMT.

One of the Herreras' planes is leaving in the morning. The message is from one of my eyes and ears on the ground who happens to work at the control tower at MEX.

I hurry up the stairs and open the door with renewed energy. Grabbing my duffle bag, I contemplate what necessities to take.

My gaze wanders over to the single small window in the space. The woman at the shrine is no longer desperately wailing for some sort of celestial affirmation. Clasping her children, she walks into the setting sun, understanding that the next phase of mourning is acceptance, followed by an unsinkable resilience to protect what is closest to your heart.

EIGHT

I adjust the square of the mirror hanging by a thin wire off a rusty nail.

My makeup is still colorful, in the style of most the Bajan women, who paint their faces in peacock blues, fuchsias, and shimmery golds—especially this time of year. Every summer, Crop Over marks the end of the sugar cane harvest. Barbados erupts into one big party, drawing tourists from all over the globe.

I grab the saline drops out of my money pouch and tilt my head back. The green contacts dry out my brown eyes, but the extra touch made it easier to look like a local and get this job. While Bonie Bozz doesn't trust anyone in his gambling room, he also wants his customers drunk and distracted. I slide a few extra pins into the edges of my light-brown afro wig and make sure the others are secured.

The tourist season brings a mixed clientele of old rich men looking to blow their time—and money—on something interesting while their wives get pampered at hotel spas, and a younger brew looking for sex and a high. The locals are more serious about their cards and dice because they have more to lose. Some of the regulars double as bodyguards, sweeping their coats aside to flash guns when needed, while others act as pushers, with everything to offer for the right price.

This is where José Herrera landed.

It didn't take me long to find him, or track his habits. Within a week, I knew where he was staying, drinking, and whoring, *and* how his suppliers were managing to get him so many pills at such low cost.

A new hospital is being built on the island, funded in part by the Herreras. A facility that will rival anything stateside. With U.S. tourists already using their vacations to take advantage of heavily discounted healthcare prices abroad, it's natural for them to do the same with drugs. Cheap opiates that sell back home for five times as much as heroin have paved the way for anyone to make a quick and profitable return on investment.

After securing cheap supplies from every crooked hospital employee dissatisfied with not making the same wages as the doctors, José cuts the opiates with heroin, amping up the street price in North America, where his concoction is most valuable.

I reach into my padded bra to lift my tits in my low-cut crop top. My belly hangs over my tight skirt, which wraps around my ass and digs into my thighs. My curves are about the only thing that still resemble me. And this is the minimum that Bonie demands of his server staff. He would like to demand more but emphasizes that he's no pimp—that stuff, the girls can do on their own time. Of course, if he traces a client from his establishment, he demands a cut.

José noticed me immediately.

As much as I'd rubbed fake tanner into my skin every morning and disguised my South African accent with a Caribbean twang, he salivated—for the same reasons the other girls down in this hot basement hate me. I'm lighter skinned, a little less plump, and a lot less desperate for money. An anomaly to their daily rhythm, and therefore a threat.

Except for Hani. Hani's a Somali girl who ended up in the Caribbean to escape charges of civil war crimes she will neither admit to nor deny. I found out I could trust her when the others tried to rough me up one night. The first time I got paid, four of them cornered me in an alley and tried to steal my earnings. Instead, I landed a swift kick to one's abdomen, broke another's nose, and pressed my forearm to one's throat until she begged for breath. Then I laughingly spared no detail about my plan to finish off every single one of them when they least expected death. As they scurried away, I threatened them some more, about what I'd do if I found out they'd told Bonie about any of this…

Hani was transfixed that night from afar—until she saw an opportunity. She demanded they hand over all *their* cash. Hani had a gun, which she later told me she'd found in the office credenza when Bonie asked her to clean the space. It was a weak story. There was no way Bonie would leave a gun around to be found by just any girl…or fail to notice it go missing.

Regardless, my co-workers didn't fuck with me again.

I don't think they'd ever fucked with Hani. Crazy was an unpredictable type of dangerous.

I wrap my fingers around the beer can balanced on the edge of the sink and tilt it towards my lips. It's like a bloody oven back here. Salty perspiration from the dimple beneath my nose mixes with the lager.

I sigh as breeze blows through a cracked window. Hardly any air circulates to the back of this place, especially the small bathroom. You could suffocate from humidity if you weren't careful.

My red lipstick is smudged. I've never been good at keeping it on, but it's part of my look—the story I sold to Bonie about visiting my family from Rio for the summer.

The Kings are a known mixed-race family on the island and own one of the larger plantations. Still, everyone has a price, especially in the form of British pounds. It didn't take much convincing to have my tracks covered by them…for as long as feasible. They'll eventually talk, but by then I will have killed José and be long gone.

I fish the cheap makeup tube out of my money pouch and circle more red along my lips.

An elbow to my ribs startles me.

"Dey waitin' for ya," says Hani in her perfect island twang before stepping next to me in front of the mirror. "If ya need anytin…I be waitin'."

I nod my thanks and exit the bathroom. I continue past a few women cleaning up the bar, towards one of only two active poker tables.

I took this earlier shift knowing that José would ask me

to play…again. And that this time I would say yes—while making him feel like I would say yes to a lot more.

Bonie doesn't like his girls involved in anything that doesn't relate to selling booze or tobacco. But I cleared it with him ahead of time by bribing him with half my winnings.

My bare skin sweats against the leather of my chair as soon as I retake my seat at the table. The blades of the fan above us grind 'cause it's old, but it makes the card room tolerable. I light up another Embassy and scan my stacks of chips. All still there.

I'm a little surprised. I took my bathroom break when I did, leaving all that money on the table, so that if anyone cheated, it would be clear it wasn't me.

As José shuffles the cards, I look at my cup of room-temperature water wishing it was filled with ice. Ice cubes are hard to come by in this rundown hotel in Bridgetown. The girl whose nose I broke walks by, asking if I need anything. I shake my head no. *I* don't trust anyone who works in this back room, either.

José Herrera takes his time, with shuffling and with observing me from across the table. His face is greasy and his hair is probably the same under his fedora. His muscles are covered by a thick layer of fat and an even thicker layer of hair. He bulges out of his short-sleeved button-up, sweat stains lining his pits and folds, his mouth clamped onto a nasty cigar. He's the kind of repulsive you wouldn't mind taking for a ride in your bed, because you could do the sorts of things with a man like that, that you would spend the rest of your life denying.

He places the shuffled cards on the table and squints at me for a lengthy moment. I throw him a flirtatious glance before playing with my fake nappy hair and turning my attention to the other three at the table. José's rotating entourage. They'd be intimidating if I hadn't spent time getting the rundown on their weaknesses. Everything from ketamine to sugar to S&M.

"There's something familiar about you," José says, shuffling the cards again like a nervous tick.

I face him and wrap my lips around my cigarette provocatively. "Hmmmm…ya wish."

"Ever been to Mexico City?"

He places the cards on the table again, peering at me as if all the booze hasn't yet blurred his vision.

I bat my long, fake lashes. "Deal da cards, a'ight?"

He shakes his head and smirks. "You need a drink to celebrate your winnings."

"We not finished yet." I haven't let José buy me a drink yet, as often as he's pressed.

"You want *more dinero*?" He raises an eyebrow. "To fix that bump in your nose?" He chuckles. "There are easier ways."

Prick.

I lean forward so he can take a good look at me and reconsider what it is he thinks he recognizes. Resting my breasts on the card table, just behind my mountain of chips, I play with the gold cross dangling from my neck.

"Speak in English, ol' man."

José swigs his drink as his companions ready themselves for any sign to jump into action.

"Hey!" Bonie yells at us. "Deal da cards!"

Bonie doesn't much care what happens to his girls outside the card room, but inside he doesn't want any trouble.

The cards land at my fingertips. I crease the edges to meet my fortune. Two of diamonds and seven of clubs. The flop will have to be good to me so I can pull off a straight.

I cup my water glass as I observe my opponents' faces. Poker is as much about psychology as it is luck. Vicente taught me that early on. There was always a box of cards on his desk.

The first time I disobeyed him as a ballsy teen, he called me into his office. I didn't know what to expect...a tongue-lashing, a beating, hard labor, or maybe he would kick me out. Nothing was off the table. He and I didn't know one another that well because I'd kept my distance.

Vicente took out the cards and shuffled them with conviction, exactly three times. Then he dealt me two and himself two. *A classic game of Texas hold 'em,* he explained, our cards face up so I could learn. Next, he dealt the cards in the middle. And then with each flip and each deal and each explanation of the rules, he told me more and more about the hand I'd been dealt and what was going through my mind. He told me how I should play, and how he knew I would play.

After the game, he issued me a warning about staying out past my curfew. I knew he knew I would try it again.

There were many more card games after that. It became our way of communicating, and my way of processing feelings about my dad's murder. I would never allow Vicente to replace my dad, but it was comforting to have a father figure. And he taught me a lot.

Which is how I know in this moment, when José turns over the first three cards, that my opponents all have better hands than me. I have two options. I can fold, or I can bluff my way into winning another round. Though their eyes are lit up, their foreheads relaxed, and their upper bodies perked, my tablemates are intimidated because of my performance all night. They're not completely confident that my lucky streak is over.

I decide to wager against the odds and ante up in the first round. I continue to call, which gives them some ease, but not for long, because when the turn comes, I raise everyone a handsome amount—knowing full well my hand is no better than theirs. A couple of them foolishly exchange glances. I've gotten under their skin. This round is mine for the taking if I continue steadfast. I look up at the clock on the wall. A bland type of clock you'd find in an old cafeteria. It's just after three in the morning. If I draw this out for too long, I'll miss my opportunity to get alone with José.

But I do like to win.

The door to the back room opens. A waft of cool air penetrating the stifling heat makes everyone sit up with uncomfortable alertness.

Bonie wouldn't let just anyone in at this hour.

The gait is light and athletic on the faded red carpet. Within moments, he's in full view, in drawstring beach pants and a tank. He puts a firm hand on José's shoulder.

"Time to go, *tío.*"

Diego's voice makes the hair on the back of my neck stand up. The identifying tattoo on his shoulder flexes.

Why the hell is he here?

I suck hard on my cigarette. I didn't want to believe Vicente when he told me Diego might be involved in all this.

And I've seen no evidence of that since my arrival weeks ago. Nothing obvious ties Diego to the operation. And yet...here he is.

He's barely glanced in my direction. He probably thinks I'm just some girl José wants to fuck.

José nods at him. "But look at all this, *sobrino*." He extends his hand to my winnings. "I'm being beat by a woman." He laughs. "We're all being beat by a woman." His entourage joins in the mirth.

My face flushes and my leg jogs under the table.

Diego's eyes lock with mine. I flick my cigarette against the ashtray to my right. I've done such a good job with my disguise, down to the colored contacts and fake crook in my nose, but Diego and I...we know each other. Intimately. I want to raise my hand to my left breast to cover my one discerning trait—a birthmark that looks like a small cow patch—but I know I've covered it with enough makeup as well.

"Wuh yuh starin' at, yuh cunt?" I snap.

Diego grits his teeth.

"Hey, Bonie—control your girl before I do!" José spits across the room. He obviously doesn't have the same regard.

Bonie struts over, glaring at me. He yanks my arm. "You been warned."

The same cold stare is dealt to José. "Last game. Finish it."

José eyes his cards and then me again, the smoke from my cigarette and his cigar acting as a shield between our mental manipulations.

I peel up the edges of my cards.

José flips the river, and...I've still got nothing.

Last round. *Fuck it.* There's more than one way to take out someone.

I raise the stakes another couple thousand. It will completely cripple my opponents.

José chomps on his cigar, contemplating, but then pushes in my raise. He's all in. And I have nothing this time. I've just thrown the man I want to kill a lifeline.

"You've played a good game, *chiquita*," he snarls. "So why lose anything? You come home with me tonight, and I'll double what you have there in your pile."

I twist my cigarette into the ashtray and place my palms on the leather edge of the poker table.

"A'ight," I say, stretching my fingers and digging my pointed acrylic red nails into the green velvet. "Put ya money where ya mout' is. Dat is twenty thousand dollars dey. Cash me out now."

José flicks a chip at me. It bounces off my pinky. "I'll give it to you how, and when, I want to, *chiquita*."

I stand up and take a few steps towards José, holding out my palm to seal the deal. The corner of my eye catches Diego's long stare.

Just then, Diego moves into position and thrusts up the edge of the table.

Cards and chips fly in all directions. José nearly falls out of his chair.

"Don mek me block wid yuh!" I scream in character, chest puffing. What I really want to do is pull off my wig and give Diego a piece of my mind.

Two of Bonie's men are immediately on either side of me.

José's entourage push Diego to the floor and reach for their weapons. But Bonie's men are faster, drawing their pistols to protect the cash as top priority. Bonie's well-armed, not about to let go of his goldmine without a fight.

Bonie summons more men and instructs them to gather the chips as he screams for me to get out. His men each grab one of my arms and escort me towards the exit.

Fuck you, Diego.

My entire body is on fire as it sinks in that I lost my opportunity to take out José, and probably this job.

On my way out, I hear the waitress whose nose I broke reprimand Bonie for hiring a crazy person.

The balmy air is refreshing. I spot an old beat-up Fiat doubling as a cab and wave at it. My pace increases and, without looking back, I step in and ride away.

Time for a new strategy.

NINE

Main Street is filled with people. Locals and tourists mixed together in a rainbow of colors as calypso music reverberates off the white-washed building walls on either side of the street. The parade moves slowly, giving everyone a chance to participate in the raucousness. Adults and kids of all ages dance and sing, the freewheeling ones drinking and smoking. Food carts pump out the local fare…rice and stew, pudding and souse, cassava pone…

I wind through the crowd in the drape of my long white skirt and matching off-the-shoulder top, bought for a few dollars from a lady at the market when I first got here. In my traditional island garb, replete with feminine ruffles, I almost blend into the festivities.

I tilt up my wide-brimmed hat as I branch onto a side street near the old hotel I haven't been back to since getting kicked out, except to have Bonie tell me he didn't want me working there anymore.

Women shouldn't be gambling, he said. Too suspicious, he said. That's why he only lets them serve drinks.

I demanded my job, or my winnings.

He wouldn't give me either. Then he told me to leave before I got escorted off the island.

I wanted to put up a fight, but since Hani is my closest thing to an ally here and in case my hunch about her relationship with Bonie is right, I didn't want to risk pissing her off.

I stop at a cart and order some cassava pone. I'm developing an addiction to the sweet dessert. Ignoring the roaches scattering up the dilapidated steps of the hotel, I hand the guy a few bills.

I'm popping the last of the cake in my mouth as Bonie descends the hotel steps. He's skinny by island standards. Not lean with bulging muscles like many of the men down here. No, he's a bag of bones covered by skin as black as night.

He retrieves a pack of smokes from the back pocket of his sagging slacks. His long fingers pop it open and stick a protruding cigarette into his mouth. It ignites a new craving in me.

I walk slowly toward the steps, wanting him to notice me first. Me—without the wig, or the makeup…Bonie has an eye for women. His bloodshot whites run across what little is exposed of my skin.

I shoot him a glance and then head towards him, my sandal landing on a concrete stair with a crack running down the center. Bonie looks surprised at my advance.

"Got an extra fag?" I ask, adding thickness to my British accent. The complete opposite of the island slang I've been perfecting.

He nods and extends the pack toward me.

I ascend a few more steps and reach daintily for a cigarette. As I place it in my mouth, he flicks his lighter.

My face nears the flame and I inhale deeply, recognizing quickly that this is not just a tobacco mix. The islanders like to cut their cigarettes with weed because it's cheaper than tobacco.

"Quite the festival," I say, looking out at the crowd as a subtle euphoria transcends my mind.

He kicks a loose rock. "Nice time to vacation."

"I've never been before. What can you recommend?"

He shrugs.

"This hotel looks like a historic landmark," I continue my small talk.

"Built by my great-grandfather," he says, surveying the tourists and locals roaming the street.

"Good line of business to be in on the island, I imagine."

Bonie turns to me with a long, penetrating gaze. "Not for a woman like ya."

I smirk. "Why do you say that?"

A couple of drunks stumble out the front door of the hotel and nearly bump into me.

"Dat be why." Bonie intercepts them and curses them out before turning back to me. "You bess be off before ya husband worries."

The paper of my spliff is burning fast and the mix makes me cough. "I don't have a husband."

As quickly as I say it, I realize I shouldn't have.

With his mouth blowing smoke rings, his eyes wander up and down my body. I'm as covered as I can be, but I may as well be naked in front of this man who knows the rules of this island better than I do. "Woman like ya?"

His gaze demands every uncomfortable truth.

"He was murdered," I say.

Bonie's eyes drift back to the street. "So ya lookin' for a new wun, hey?"

A smaller parade has branched off from the one on Main Street. It's coming our way, and a commotion has erupted.

I don't answer, and instead focus on the group of men and women in vibrant, scant costumes who are singing and dancing, blissfully detached from the doldrums of everyday life. I want to leap from the steps and join them…but then they've passed, almost as quickly as they appeared. The street is again at a regular hum.

Bonie lets out a hollow laugh. "Young an foolish, like ya."

His gaze shifts back to me as I flick off some ash into nearby dirt.

"Dat black car be parked here for a week now," he says.

I look over my shoulder at what he's referring to. It's a black SUV. Hard to tell whether anyone's in it because the windows are tinted.

Something about the vehicle seems out of place, even though the island is filled with this type of luxury transportation. Maybe because it doesn't have the typical obnoxious foreigners hanging out the windows making a ruckus.

"Maybe ya uncle is worried about where ya spendin' time." Bonie pauses. "Or maybe someone else is." He says this slowly, so I can absorb every word.

The lump in my throat is hard to swallow. I can't face Bonie because I have nothing to say. I'm abruptly aware that this island, even with all its tourists, is a lot smaller than I want it to be. Aware that every strategy I came with is losing legs and that even escaping alive may not be possible.

"Thanks for the fag" is what I muster before dropping it and twisting my sandal over the smoke.

Bonie throws his spliff into the street and walks back up the stairs into his hotel.

I creep close enough to the SUV to register the license plate.

TEN

The Lincoln Town Car pulls up to hotel registration at the Turtle Beach resort. Moments later, the driver is opening my door. I take his hand, extending my long red acrylic nails that match the tight red dress I snugged my way into. My large afro wig bumps against the car door as my heel plants on the walkway that leads to the hotel. I'm back in my alias getup.

"I'll see you in there," I tell the driver.

He nods and shuts the door.

The humidity is more obvious now that the wind has calmed. A welcome breeze cools my face, drenched in makeup I fear will melt off. I tuck my purse tightly under my arm, the outline of my piece inside it pressing into my armpit.

This is where the local works. The local whose name came up associated with the license plate from earlier today. The SUV is registered to a car service on the island. One that supposedly shuttles a security guard who works at one of the most exclusive resorts on Barbados.

In the distance, a reggae band plays to a large-forming crowd.

When I called the hotel looking for the guard, I found out about a private party here tonight, another part of Crop Over festivities. One of many private parties on the island, but this particular soirée has one of two guests confirmed that I inquired about. José Herrera is slated to attend—without his nephew. Apparently José has tired of mixing with the locals in the underbelly of Bridgetown. Or, more likely, he's coming to score more clients or expand his distribution network, or both.

Walking towards the music, I catch all the attention a tall woman with curves would. They can't tell whether I'm some older man's arm candy or a whore.

I lift my chin. *Primitive thinking.*

The open venue smells of saltwater as the ocean waves slap gently against the shore. I nudge my way to the front of a bar to order a rum cocktail, throwing just enough money on the bar before being shoved to the side by an already drunk British couple. My drink sloshes as I my eyes scan the room.

He's here somewhere…

An obese white man begs me to join him on the dance floor, but I shake my head and gyrate to the rhythm instead, playing the part, teasing. Several beautiful locals, their black muscles bulging, bump up against me as they jam to the heavy bass.

Bopping to the beat in amusement, I keep walking past the main stage of the event…past a couple singers, a few musicians, a DJ…to the rear of the hotel where there's a quieter lounge.

That's where I spot him.

He's all dolled up, talking with a ring of men who look like they'd be in suits if they weren't on an island. For José "dolled up" means a clean shirt, though still ill-fitting.

I strut by him, close enough for him to look up. His eyes widen and his cigar falls limp in his mouth. His conversation reels to a halt as he lifts his hand to signal to somebody.

The entire table shifts their view, but I keep walking until I grab a seat next to my driver who is where I asked him to be but doesn't look much like a driver anymore. He looks more like a pimp, which is exactly the role I told him to dress for.

I wrap my arms around him and whisper in his ear, "When I head to the bathroom, I want you to offer me to that man wearing a blue-striped shirt. The only one smoking a cigar."

As we confirm the rest of the plan, I additionally point out José's entourage seated across the wide bar from us.

Swirling the ice cubes in my glass, I glance back at José. He's conversing again but keeps looking in my direction. I snuggle closer to my driver. His cronies murmur in a low hum as they, too, keep their attention on me.

Crunching on one of a few ice cubes remaining, I grin in the face of the devil before standing up to walk to the bathroom.

My heels click on the marble floor as I make my way back through the growing crowd. Rubbing against bodies, my dress binds me tighter as my fingers clench around my clutch. I'm just out of José's sight, when—

A large hand grips my arm. The outline of a gun barrel pinches my side. I'm thrust by one large black man into the chest of another large black man who rips my purse from under my arm. I don't recognize either of them, but I do recognize that they're not looking to party.

The men are dressed not in light resort wear but dark suits. One bends his head close to my ear and tells me to follow him. The accent is local. *Would José hire local thugs to off me?*

We weave swiftly through the crowd and exit on the ocean side of the hotel. The beach is sparsely populated by tourists and no one who looks like a resort employee.

Heels in the sand trip me up, but if I struggle or scream, I'm sure they'll take me out quickly. Those guns have silencers. I know how this bidding is done and I curse myself for not planning ahead for…this possibility.

The adrenaline pumping through my veins is sobering. The gun in my bag is gone, and the gun inside the thin holster around my thigh…doesn't have nearly a large enough magazine to be a threat. Still, it's better than nothing.

We reach a road a few blocks from the resort, and a black SUV. The license plate confirms it's the one from earlier.

The men escort me towards the rear door. Before opening the car, one of them holds back my arms while the other pats me down. Detecting my weapon, he bends down to my thigh and grips it. I kick swiftly, aiming for his side but hoping for his head. My dress rips loudly. He retracts a bit, not having expected the assault. I continue kicking as I try to pull out of his partner's grip, but my reflexes are sluggish, my dress is still too tight, and my heels are putting me off-balance. He grabs my leg before my next kick lands.

His eyes burning into mine and sweat forming on his brow, he deftly reaches up my skirt to pull off my holster.

These are professionals—not simple island thugs.

The rear door of the SUV opens and they throw me inside.

I land on soft leather cushions. When I catch my breath and look up…

His attire is white and loose, and on his dark skin… dramatic. His head is cocked upwards, with enough hair falling over his dark eyes to screen his emotions. The hard line of his jaw flexes.

Diego.

The thought of him being behind this had run through my mind, but the plausibility seemed remote. He's staying on a different part of the island, and aside from the one time at Bonie's, he hadn't left his resort—not even to visit the hospital his family is helping fund. He held a couple of meetings at his hotel with government types, but that was to be expected.

What I wasn't expecting was to see him now, sitting on the bench seat opposite me.

"If you wanted to see me so badly, you could've just asked me out on a date."

I carefully begin pulling pins from my wig so that I can pull the whole mess from my head.

"Red is not my favorite color on you, Victoria," he says, knocking on the solid partition separating the driver of the vehicle from the backseat.

"Kidnapper is not a good look on you, Diego."

The engine rumbles to life.

"How soon did you know it was me in that room, at Bonie's?" I ask casually, this being our first chance to discuss the poker game gone awry.

He smirks. "You're the only person I've seen take such big risks at a poker table."

I yank off the wig and then straighten the rip in my dress, which stops just below my crotch.

He inhales sharply.

"I should have played him earlier," I remark. "It was a mistake to wait."

Diego's expression turns dead-serious. "It was a bigger mistake coming to Barbados to get to my uncle."

There's not enough air circulating. I try to lower the window, but it's locked.

Frustrated, I pick at the fake bump in my nose until it peels and breaks off.

"He's getting protection from you," I retort. "What's there to worry about?"

Diego sits back and raises the wingspan of his arms to rest atop the seat. His loose button-up untucks from his linen pants.

"Have you been over here this entire time since leaving the ranch?" he asks.

I pull at the top of my dress, which sticks to my skin uncomfortably. Diego's gaze lingers at my breasts.

"I'm sure you already know the answer to that question," I say.

He offers me a bottle of water from the small stash cradled in the side pocket of the back door.

"Don't fuck with me, Victoria. You know everyone from the authorities to the *cholos* have been talking about you— your family. And not saying very nice things."

I crank the plastic top off the bottle. Slowly enveloping my mouth around it, I tilt my head back to gulp down some relief.

"Since when do I care what people say about me?" I let out an exaggerated sigh and wipe the excess water from my lips.

Diego continues to regard me like a scolding parent.

"There's no record of you entering Barbados. You're using a fake travel document. But then one of José's men saw you out of your…getup, on a local plantation. I had no idea you had any interest in…sugar."

I smooth down a few out-of-place strands of hair, the bun I'd had under the wig a loose mess.

"I had no idea your family had any interest in building a hospital," I respond. "And all the way over here, in the Caribbean. How valiant." I flick my fake nails against one another. "Except you *know* what your uncle's been doing while you've been trying to help the islanders." One of the bright red nails falls off. "Word on the street is he's got a monopoly over the marketplace for his type of 'painkiller.'"

Diego's face is unflinching. "Building the hospital will put an end to it."

Diego thinks he knows as much as I do, so he only sees me as being in the way.

"Did you also think that investing in pharmaceuticals would put an end to it?" I counter.

His jaw stiffens. "Teresa was developing a drug to help get people off opiates."

My eyes lock with his. "How ironic."

He smacks the seat with a fist. "Stay away from José. This is not your problem. It's *ours*. The Herreras."

I place the cool water bottle against my neck. "I'm just here to make deals for some sugar transport. For the Morenos."

Diego lunges towards me, grasping at the straps of my dress. I gasp at his sudden nearness.

"I'm fucking serious, Victoria. José isn't some *malandro* with no family, friends, history, or name. He isn't Teresa." He lets go. "You should never have gotten involved with…this."

He grunts and slides me into the corner. His face is as close to mine as it's ever been without us breaking into a passionate kiss.

"José is the second in command." He grips my shoulder. "In *my* family."

Pressed between the hard leather and Diego's hard torso, I can't decide whether this is an invitation to fight him or fuck him.

My breathing hastens.

"That's not what *I* heard," I tell him. "I heard he lost that position, which is why he's turned against your family."

Diego tugs again at my dress straps, his knuckles digging into my chest, until one of them breaks.

"They *will* kill you, eventually," he urges. "You know this."

I attempt to create some space, but my struggles just intertwine us more.

His hand wanders into my hair and breaks loose the band holding the knot. I breathe in the familiar musky scent of his neck as his face burrows in the dark-brown waves.

"Do you understand me?" he pleads. "They will do it without checking in with me. They will do it despite what I say or do to defend you. And once they decide, they will do it so swiftly. You won't have a chance to reach for your weapon of choice—like tonight. You won't be able to outmaneuver or outthink. You will just be dead."

The seam of the seat digs into me, my emotions hanging off the edge of a cliff. My hand fumbles for balance until it lands on the thick, hard outline of his cock. A jolt of heat shoots through me.

Diego reaches around my ass and slides me further underneath him.

I lock my thighs around him, the dress tearing further as the SUV continues to rumble. He pulls down the top of my dress exposing a round breast. My nipple is already pert in anticipation of his hot breath and flicking tongue.

When he performs just that, my hips circle beneath him. My moan is no longer silent. His stiff cock grinds into the last few layers of fabric between us as he sucks fervently at my nipple and I twist a lock of his hair between my fingers. The muscles of his back ripple as he pulls me tighter into him, trying to mold us into one. My pussy pulses to the rhythm of his insistence.

He looks up with his big, dark eyes, trying to figure out how to quell a storm he can't control. His thumb draws across my lips.

"Stay away from José," he begs. "Promise me."

I bite at it, locking it briefly between my teeth.

"You took away my guns tonight because you don't trust me," I remind him. "Why would you want me to commit to anything?"

Fingers reach the thin silk of my panties and he cups that spot that's already plump, wet, ready.

"You're so sure of yourself, Victoria, but I could have driven you anywhere. Right up to José's door. You know that's what he expects me to do."

My fingers untie the drawstring of his pants. "What's stopping you?"

His erection pops out as his fingers move the fabric of my underwear to one side and he enters me swiftly. I gasp.

"A belief that you will come…" He glides deeper. "To your senses."

His hips grind into mine, hitting all those spots that render me in a state more euphoric than any other mélange could. My body is insensibly wrapped around his. I grip on tightly, nails digging, mouth gasping, and pressure building to just that right amount. My moaning turns into a low wail as a wave of sweet nectar releases from my core and rolls through my body like thunder.

As I'm coming off my orgasm, his thrusts get more fiercely determined. He's ready to come and my body meets his in every arch, curl, and undulation so that he can get there.

His release courses through him and he collapses on top of me. Clothes rumpled, slick skin sticking to one another, our hearts pound in unison.

But then he props himself up and we begin to unravel.

Within moments, we're on opposite sides of the bench again. The low hum of the engine gets louder in my ears and every slight bump and turn jars me back to a reality that's not focused on my tainted desires.

We reach an area with lights and I lean over to peer out the window. A familiar line of mahogany trees leads to the entrance of a plantation house. I should have known he knows where I'm staying.

Palm pressed against the windowpane, I count the vehicles to determine whether I have any visitors…

Five. Like Always.

"Don't think I'll do your bidding," I warn, "just because of our…physical relationship."

"That's all this is to you—a physical relationship?"

Diego's voice is distant in my mind, overshadowed by the burning questions about how much the rest of his family knows about my stay in Barbados.

"We both got what we wanted," I say. "And if you hadn't interfered tonight—and hadn't interfered at Bonie's—we both would have gotten more. Now let me out."

Diego knocks a different pattern on the driver's partition and the SUV rolls to a stop. Locks unclick as I reach for a handle.

"Ten cuidado, mi amor," he says.

I step out into the night, not looking back.

ELEVEN

José is leaving the island. Like we all want to leave. We've been at everything for too long here and it's feeling cramped. Everywhere you go you recognize the same details, and people recognize you.

He's departing tomorrow by helicopter, from the same discreet landing strip he arrived at, on the east side of the island out near the old Ebworth plantation. The place is damn near abandoned, except for a few squatters occupying some rundown hangars.

But before he goes, he has one last shipment to secure, one last deal to make. And he's doing it at the hospital construction site. Tonight.

Sundown on the island is often pitch black. But the moon is hanging big in the sky right now, making the construction site an even more well-lit mess. Illuminating the hiding places that can hurt or expose you if you aren't careful. If the security lights catch you at the wrong angle.

They've constructed the wood frame structure that's intended to become a garage for EMS vehicles. But it's currently being used by José to store boxes that look like janitorial supplies but are really the pharmaceutical ingredients for his opiate cocktail.

I plod through the dust, wood chips, and nails littering the ground, with two sets of PVC pipes tucked under my arm and a rifle secured at my back by a strap across my chest. I'm only about fifty feet from where José and a crew of five have gathered.

Every now and then I hear a burst of laughter. They're celebrating. They've shipped off more supplies this trip than on their last visit. But they're also discussing relocating their operations. Police are coming around, and construction on the hospital will finish in less than a year.

I crouch at the entrance to the garage, and place one of the pipes near a stack of plywood. After double-checking that the wiring and stripped-down flip phone are secured to the PVC, I push my slipping rifle back up on to my shoulder and then shuffle backwards, further into the room.

With my breathing hurried and perspiration pouring down my back and chest, I place the second set of strewn-together pipes by a garbage can next to the janitorial boxes I envision José and his men rushing to survey when they detect a problem.

There's no disguising intentions anymore.

After a final check of my own corresponding flip phone to ensure I've programmed the correct number for each explosive, I look up towards scaffolding about a hundred feet away, which leads to two more levels.

That's the spot, for now.

The muscles of my arms cramp from climbing to a high enough lookout point. High enough to not be noticed but close enough to hit my targets. It's bloody hot up here, with almost no ventilation, but this is where I'm going to wait.

Hunched beneath a pane-less window, I'm grateful for the one tall light outside that illuminates enough of the area for me to gauge the activity below. The barrel of my rifle rests on the window cutout as I stare through the scope, hoping the details of my plan are on point.

It's time.

I retrieve the flip phone from my vest pocket and my thumb presses the numbers linked to the first bomb at the entrance. Barely a full ring later, the explosion rocks the landing I'm stationed on like a four-magnitude earthquake near a fault line. A dust of plaster covers my skin and clothes.

It's done. I cough and cover my mouth as I await their arrival. As their muffled voices increase in volume, I hear one of the men shout that he's spotted me.

Shit.

The group disperses, four going further into the structure, two cursing about coming after me.

Stowing my phone, I wipe sweaty hands on my soot-covered pants, reposition my rifle, and aim at the first backside that comes into focus. I shoot…and miss.

I need to make this fucking shot.

Eyes squinting through the scope, palms gripping the steel, I pull back the trigger again.

The bullet blasts right through the center of the man's back. He goes down and he goes down fast. I retreat from the window frame, breathing like I've just been on a treadmill, and reach again for the flip phone.

The second bomb is bigger. It shakes and rattles the structure we're in, hard. The landing I'm on cracks, and more debris invades my eyes, mouth, and lungs. It's suffocating.

Bullets and footsteps near. I have to move.

Grasping a beam, I flex my body around shots being fired, ignoring the splinters digging into my fingers. I finally find reprieve behind a mocked-together wall.

My eyes blink a few times to focus before I scan the scene and shoot back. I won't be able to hold off whoever it is for long.

I know there are stairs…

Slinging the rifle over my shoulder, I grab a metal pipe and, with all my tired body weight, use it to launch myself across a gap in the flooring towards a makeshift set of stairs. I land hard. The steps resonate beneath me as I run down them and take a sharp right to avoid a bullet that whizzes by my head.

I won't die without knowing I've killed José.

Dust hangs over the construction site like a morning fog. I plant and do a one-eighty just as one of José's men rounds the corner and fires. A bullet skins my forearm as I cock my rifle. There's no time to aim, so I pull the trigger from the hip like an amateur. It lands just below the thug's groin and tears his thigh, anyway. He won't stop screaming, so I hit the top of his chest to finish him.

I spot a trailer twenty feet away. As I scamper towards it, an eerie silence engulfs the area. Like the silence I imagine engulfs you when you know that you're at death's door.

I try the trailer door. It's locked. I smack my palm at it, trying to count the executions in my head, and then heave my entire body, holding my forearm tight against my vest in an attempt to stop the bleeding.

The door still won't open. I take a few steps back, point my gun at the knob, and pull the trigger.

Nothing. I'm out of ammo.

I pat at the belt around my waist for the extra magazine… but it's gone.

Fuck.

I bust the handle of my gun through the small window in the door. The shattering glass pierces the air.

I thrust my arm through the cramped space, shards of glass cutting my skin, until I find the deadbolt and twist it open. Tossing my gun on a couch that lines one wall, I scan for another weapon. A gas-powered chainsaw. I grab it and then slither next to a filing cabinet and wait. My arms look like I've been wrestling a hyena.

The door to the trailer creaks open.

"Victoria!" a raspy voice calls out. A voice that's smoked too many cigars and drunk too much hard liquor. It's José. That he and I are the last ones left on the battlefield is poetic.

He calls out my name a few more times, like we're personal friends and I've unhinged for no good reason. An aberration no one expected, like snow falling in summer.

Infested with splinters and bloodied with cuts, my throbbing fingers tighten around the pull string as he walks through the open door. I call back at him as the chainsaw roars to life, hoisting it above my head…

As the shadow of José's body nears, I slam down the chainsaw. I have no idea whether I've missed or beheaded him until he screams out and his gun falls to the floor.

The chainsaw continues buzzing in an otherwise-still background, like a simmering stew drowning out the last of my tired sanity. I switch it off.

Still on his knees, José grasps for the gun. But my stretched-out leg is quicker. I kick the weapon to the other side of the trailer, far from both our reaches.

"I should have killed you in Vegas." José's voice is strained. He's now flat on his stomach, unmoving. "I could have. But…Diego…" He rolls, grasping his blood-drenched midsection. "I warned him…for years…that you would be his downfall. But you had something he wanted, so desperately." He coughs. "Some special tits and pussy."

I walk out from beside the filing cabinet and stare at the damage I've inflicted.

José is clasping an almost-detached hand. Shrapnel from one of the bombs has cut his head and neck, and his clothing is tattered down his entire red-stained side. I stand in front of him, knowing how easy it will be to finish him off.

"There's no reason to kill me anymore, Victoria."

José's statement startles me. His eyes pin mine, as if he's reading my mind. "Your mother finally did it. She's dead."

My chest tightens, as though my lungs can't expand enough to get air. My muscles liquefy and the chainsaw slips from my hand. I grasp the edge of a desk next to me.

He's lying. I would have found out from someone else. Not like this, not from José.

"It's true," he says with a steady voice. "While you've been busy getting into my business here in Barbados, your mother managed to end her misery with that *maricón,* in Mexico."

I just talked to Vicente. Why wouldn't he have said anything?

My mind scans for the last conversation I can remember having with my mother. It was right before I left for Barbados. She knew I had killed Teresa, and she was worried for my safety. She wasn't sure either Vicente or Diego could protect me anymore.

I told her to focus on rehabilitation. That I needed her to stay alive, for me. That it's what my father would have wanted.

"You act like a child, Victoria." José's voice fills the room again and I look down at him, writhing and helpless yet still so goddamned sure of himself. "This business will go on, even flourish, with or without me. There's too much demand, on an international level. But Diego…as soon as my men find out that you killed me…he will be killed. The way Renaldo was."

His uttering of Renaldo's name sends a fire through my chest and makes me want to dig my keys into his eye socket.

My boot inches closer to one of his wounds.

He swats at it with his good hand, but I push myself off the desk and stomp on the bloodied limb. And stomp, and stomp, and stomp. I keep stomping while he cries out, cursing me and the Morenos, until I can't breathe or see through my wet eyes. I hunker over, palms on my knees, as if about to heave.

"Don't be unreasonable and make another mistake." José continues to negotiate and cloud my mind.

Hands shaking, I dig out my pack of cigarettes and lighter from a zippered pocket in my pants.

He's lying. About my mother, and especially about Diego. The Herreras will protect Diego's life with everything they have. They would never allow him to get killed. Then again, they allowed José's business to flourish, so maybe they don't have as much control as I thought they did.

"I saw how you killed my man in Vegas and then Teresa. And now,"—he sweeps his hand around—"all this."

His hand reaches upward with certainty that I'll grasp onto it.

"So much determination," he continues. "It's impressive. There are business opportunities that you, and I, can dominate. You don't have to be just…a killer, working simple jobs for Vicente. He doesn't appreciate your talent. I will make you a real boss, and you and Diego can stop living in the shadows of your love affair. I know it's what you both want."

Flipping open the pack, I shake it a few times until a cigarette pops out. The blood is coagulating on my forearms. I touch the spongy mess.

Lighting up my smoke, I turn and walk away from José. The nicotine hits my lungs like a comforting plush toy. I sit on the long couch, crossing my legs and swiping away the soot that's piled on my clothes and skin.

Bleeding out can cause a man to get desperate, but if José's not lying… I take another deep inhale of my cigarette and let the ash fall on the filthy stack of folders piled on the cushion next to me.

He's offering me a truce to the war that I've created. A war that started with the death of my father. Crooked men, and all their opportunistic lies. The only time I've felt any purpose is when I've been destroying them. Except there will never be peace amongst men like José.

"You overestimate my loyalty to Diego," I finally respond, standing and reaching for a lineman's axe resting against the wall. The cig drops from my mouth.

I lunge at José. Swinging with a sea of red before my eyes, I know I have more than the advantage that I need to decapitate the man I've been trying to kill.

Half the battle is having the guts to do it.

TWELVE

I twist the throttle of my satin black Ducati, shifting up as I hit Hwy 2A North.

I haven't slept, and the adrenaline pumping through my veins earlier has worn off and been replaced by a throbbing pain throughout my entire body.

The sun is higher in the sky than I want it to be. I'd hoped to leave at sunrise—meeting Vicente at the same obscure air strip I landed at and taking off for Mexico City. But there was more clean-up than I expected. The trailer was like the site of a massacre.

Vicente was my first call after killing José. I demanded to know what had happened to my mother, screaming at him through the phone even though I knew my outburst was dangerous. Dawn had broken and someone was bound to start milling about, even on a Sunday.

He told me she had returned from the rehab center in good spirits and then last weekend went away to the spa. That wasn't unusual. But that's where they found her in her room one morning when she didn't make her scheduled massage. Apparently she'd lied to him about her state of mind.

He told me he's already planned an appropriately traditional church funeral at the Catedral Metropolitana. He insists that's what she'd want even though my mother was never a devout Catholic. He also informed me that the official story of her death being released to the media is an unexpected heart attack.

All their friends are in mourning, he said. *Their friends.* As if they've still been that couple who rolls with the in crowd, going out every Friday and Saturday to the hottest events and then brunching every Sunday to wash away their hangovers. That hasn't happened in years.

I grip the handlebars tighter as I weave around a pickup truck like it's nothing more than a pylon on an obstacle course. My speedometer inches towards a hundred.

I told him I needed to get out of Barbados, and quick. That's when he told me he was already on the island. When he couldn't get a hold of me last week, he flew in and went to the plantation where I told him I would be. But the Kings hadn't seen me in over a week.

Of course not. Too many people were looking for me. After Diego dropped me off, I immediately pulled a favor from my only other ally and began staying with Hani.

I told Vicente I would meet him at the airstrip by noon—
but if I didn't arrive, not to look for me and to leave Barbados.
Then I cut the call, packed José's body into my SUV, and
drove to the incineration plant.

As I pushed José into the fire and watched his limbs
smolder into oblivion, I obsessed over whether my prolonged
absence caused my mother's death. Just as I'd obsessed over
whether my inability to stop my father from going to work in
the textile factory that one day...

The dirty brown mass of an animal darts in front of my
motorcycle. I curse into my helmet as I swerve, this time
less elegantly, RPMs screaming as my downshift sends my
speedometer plummeting and my bike leans at a deadly angle.
My boots and jeans scrape the pavement while my upper
body strains in the opposite direction, trying to defy the law
of gravity...

My rear tire catches the gravel off the highway's edge as
I grind to a near halt just in time to prevent an ugly spin and
even uglier accident.

When I look up, the coyote-like dog is trotting away. It
looks back, obviously as startled as me. I straighten my bike,
heart pounding and sweat trickling down my forehead like it's
last night, and accelerate again down the highway.

Renaldo's funeral was at the Catedral. It was attended by
every dignitary in Mexico City, with fans turning out in mobs
so massive, they had to block off every street leading to the
church, and enforce the barricades with tight security.

There'd been expectations. That I would give a heartfelt
speech like Renaldo's coach and father, or sit in the front pew

reserved for close family, wearing a dark veil and wailing like Renaldo's mother and four sisters. I did neither.

I had met Renaldo's family just once, and their cool reception left me suspecting that their paramount concern was whether Renaldo's marrying me would put an end to their gravy train. They had devoted their life to Renaldo's success, his mother let slip over dessert, while I was very young and lacked the family values of a Latina. His mother would eventually adore me, Renaldo assured, but we'd never gotten there. She nodded in my direction at the Catedral before clasping onto one of his ex-girlfriends.

The video I'd spent that morning watching drowned out the mass and allowed me to escape the claustrophobic trap of the church around me. It was of Renaldo and me, made shortly before he left on his sailing trip.

I was in his kitchen, clad in just my thong and one of his tanks—dehydrated. It was late afternoon, and we'd just had sex in a leisurely way, knowing we wouldn't see each other for a week.

Having just gotten a new iPad, he wanted to capture me in action on it, so he could watch me when he was away. I warned him, pointing my finger into the camera, my other fingers clasped around a water bottle, that if I ever found out he had shown this video to anyone, I would…murder him.

He told me to be quiet and to pour the rest of the water down the front of my tank.

"What's in it for me?" I asked, licking my lips as I questioned the camera.

"I'll make you come again," he answered before moving out from behind the iPad as I enacted his request.

The icy water startled my skin, hardening my nipples as the wet cotton clung to my full breasts. He walked towards me, dropped to his knees, and moved my thong to one side. As his tongue flicked at my sensitive nub, his hands wandered freely. My fingers gripped his hair as he cupped my ass, before parting my cheeks and playing with the creases that led to my wet opening. I closed my eyes, forgetting about the electronic device on the stand in front of us as I succumbed to him in every way, eventually toppling over him and taking in his hardness.

That video captured the sexual electricity that fueled our relationship and I couldn't stop thinking about that during the depressing mass.

I back off the throttle of the Ducati, shifting down to make a hard right onto a narrow dirt road that leads to a paved runway not many know exists. Forty miles north of Bridgetown puts the private airstrip smack in the middle of a desolate grassy jungle.

Diego attended the funeral, seated in the row reserved for the entire Herrera family, opposite from the Morenos. Opposite me. Guilt washed over me for having agreed to meet with him while Renaldo was gone, even if only to defend the choice I'd made. Followed by anger, because Diego had made me doubt my decision, even though I'd played it off confidently.

Our gazes met as the priest delivered the Lord's Prayer, hitting the line about resisting temptation.

"*No nos dejes caer en tentación y líbranos del mal.*"

Turning away, I pushed past the people next to me in the pew and standing along the sidelines, swimming through stares and whispers until I found a confessional. I slipped inside and voiced my act of contrition into the empty darkness as the choir sang to the angels watching over us.

Nearing the row of a half-dozen corrugated metal hangers lining the asphalt runway, I spot Vicente's Embraer 450. It's not the biggest jet he could own, but it has a relatively short takeoff distance and a long enough range to get him from anywhere in the Americas to Mexico City in under four hours.

Vicente has always been practical like that.

Even when I was young, he raised me without unnecessary conversation or theories about life. He's always valued decisiveness and loyalty. When I took the job flying small cargo for his transport company, he told me that if I was ever uncomfortable doing something he asked of me, to quit rather than question. But I never questioned him—nor quit. Not when the deliveries were obviously not banknotes, not when he sent me to Cuba with a gun and fake papers to pick up a shipment of animal pelts, and not when he told me to confirm José Herrera's dealings with a cartel in Barbados.

I swing my leg over the Ducati, my black jeans sticking to me from riding for over an hour in the heat and humidity. My helmet is damn near suffocating, and I struggle to remove it, my hair clinging to it like coarse tread. It finally pops off and drops to the ground.

I'm soaked in sweat beneath my black leather riding jacket, and I fling it off to breathe easier. I stretch my arms above my head, letting the slight breeze rustle my white t-shirt. In the distance, I can hear the roar of a lone truck barreling down the highway. Not a lot of traffic in these parts, especially on a Sunday.

Unburdened of my gear, my chest still feels heavy, like I've been sucking in a miserable amount of dust. I swipe a strand of hair sticking to my cheek, and then reach back down for my helmet and jacket. Tucking them under one arm, I head toward the aircraft, continuing my survey with each stride and calling out Vicente's name.

A few single-engine airplanes that look like they haven't been flown in years speckle the apron, and one King Air, its twin engines glistening in the unforgiving sun. The last time I flew one of those, I was delivering bank notes for the Banco de México and my plane got hijacked.

My boots kick loose stones in the dirt as I continue towards the King Air, my pulse racing from the memory. I was young, and not expecting a gun at my back shortly after landing. In turn, they weren't expecting a girl and started laughing. One of the three waved off the other two and told them he had it covered, his intentions clear as he ground his tongue between his teeth.

I bolted back into my plane and he followed, tumbling on top of me and hissing threats. But my hand reached the gun under the seat faster than he expected, as I simultaneously threw a knee into his crotch and a thumb into an eye socket. The squishy mess dripped down my left hand as my right one pointed the gun into his gut and pulled the trigger.

It was the first time I killed someone.

I likened it to taking down a lion in the savannah. If the contest had been determined by sheer mass, I would have lost, but with training and a gun, anything was possible.

My hand shakes against the white-painted aluminum as I let out a deep breath and turn away from the plane. Looking back at Vicente's jet, I call out his name again without getting a response.

That's odd. He told me he would meet me here…unless something's changed.

I grab my phone out of my back pocket and scan it for messages. *None.*

My thoughts grind to a halt when I notice one other fragment of the scenery. A dirt bike covered in dust. Parked near the closest hangar, it's out of a place, like a puzzle piece in the wrong box. The wind picks up as I walk towards it, whipping around me like a blow dryer.

Whoever else is here arrived by a back route, off the main arteries, and long ago enough for me to not notice. The engine's not clicking, and when I lightly touch the exhaust the metal is warm but not hot. I gauge that the bike and whoever rode it have been here an hour, maybe more.

Backing up a few steps, I stop at a door handle—but not before considering not stopping at all.

I look back at the jet. It's eerily motionless. No signs of a flight crew. No usual preflight checklists underway. And definitely no sign of Vicente.

They're hell-bent on killing me now, I'm sure. Unless I kill them first. I pull out my Glock and check the cartridge. *Seven shots.* I shove the gun back in my hip holster and crank the door handle to step inside the hangar.

Instead of aircraft, the place is packed with old relics. Stacks of dusty plantation tools, large car repair machinery, a dilapidated piano set in a corner next to some vintage kitchen appliances, and bookshelves brimming with American reading material. I wade through boxes to an opening that's been cleared just of enough junk to host a chair, with a man roped to its wooden limbs. *Vicente.*

His head is drooped, with dried blood plastered to his hairline, nose, and cracked lips. His attire is as dusty as the items surrounding him, with one jacket sleeve ripped off to expose a deep wound.

I lift his head by a crop of grey hair. *He's alive.*

He attempts to focus, but it's obvious he already put up a fight, and lost. It wouldn't take a lot to lose in this wasteland.

He mouths my name like a prayer—for salvation, for loyalty.

I grab my canteen and pour the water over his head, making sure enough drops land in his mouth to give him that hope. The old man is a father to me, regardless of our turbulent past.

Feet shuffling from behind another stack of junk divert my attention.

He's not dressed in a tuxedo, cruising a casino, nor is he lying naked in my bed. But he's got an expression on his face that I've seen before. Not a look of victory or satisfaction, but simply determination.

One hand tugs on the faded red bandana around his neck while the other grips his pistol. His biceps pop around the sleeves of his black t-shirt.

"How'd you find him here?" I inquire, checking the holster strapped to my hip.

He takes a few steps towards the chair and places a firm grip on Vicente's shoulder.

"I'm sure you know Vicente has a thing for young, attractive men." He digs into the bloody wound on Vicente's shoulder until Vicente yelps out. "They're not too hard to find on this island—or persuade."

It was Vicente's dirty secret. I'd walked in on it once, and I know he saw me. For a long time, I wondered how my mother put up with it, until I lost Renaldo and realized we all deal with loss in different ways. And our private urges.

In so many ways, Vicente was untouchable. But it's our weaknesses that ultimately bring us down.

"I would've killed him already, but I wanted to wait for you." Diego steps back to take in the father-daughter sight. "I wanted you to see how serious my offer was in Vegas."

Vicente looks up at me through swollen eyes. He knows I've been lying about the rumors. Rumors that started as quickly as my and Diego's love affair that night in the taqueria, when someone recognized us and snapped a picture of us leaving together. Rumors fueled by Diego's insistence on having me.

When we were in Croatia, Diego told me that he would die before giving up on me.

I told him he was confusing obsession with commitment, before resting my foot in his crotch and taking another sip of my bitter Americano while a light sea breeze delighted my face. He grew hard again even though we'd just finished making love instead of eating the breakfast sent up to us by the café owner.

Our appetite for one another was ferocious.

I brush sweat off my forehead with my palm. "It won't change anything between us. I won't commit to anything. And this will be just a trophy kill for you, with no basis but revenge."

"Like my uncle was for you." He pulls back the hammer of his gun. "So we'll be even."

"No!" I yell, trying to stop what could set in motion a bloodier war. "We're even already. It *was* revenge—for killing my mother."

Diego's eye twitches. Apparently this is news to him as well.

"You know your uncle was double-dealing here," I say. "Orchestrating smuggle routes so the cartel can push through opiates into North America. All in the name of helping build a hospital to save the people he was killing."

"I told you that executing him was not your decision to make," Diego seethes, glaring at me and then at Vicente.

"It was what I needed to do." Sweat drips into my eyes, stinging.

"How can I trust anything between us now?" His finger is still on the trigger.

"You told me you weren't involved with your uncle in any way, yet you showed up in Barbados. How can I trust anything *you* say?"

There's no more time to debate. My foot kicks in a circular motion, knocking the pistol out of Diego's hand. His mouth opens in surprise and then turns upwards into an uncomfortable grin.

"I told you I was negotiating with the hospital," he says. "Trying to fix the mess instead of making it worse—which is what you and Vicente just did."

Rapid breaths escape through Diego's nose—snorts of disbelief and anguish—before he lunges at me and knocks me over. My back smacks against the cement floor, the thud reverberating through my torso…just like the realization that I may not be right or able to control everything in my life.

Diego's weight on top of me is familiar…his breath at my ear, his thighs between mine…but this time he's not trying to seduce me.

"Vicente's an old man making bad decisions," he says, "and he's dragging you into the middle. I know you won't kill him, so I will. And walk away from everything." His attention darts towards his gun, lying just a few feet away. "Including you."

The air is so thick—like syrup hardening over my lungs. One palm sweats at his chest trying to fight him off, while the other hovers at my hip over the trigger of my gun.

He rolls off of me towards the weapon on the ground, and reaches it.

"You don't care about Victoria," he spits at Vicente. "You want a reason to get rid of me because our relationship is a weakness to your organization."

He levels his gun at Vicente. But at the same time, I pull out mine.

I'm panting, but regain focus and plant one palm on the dusty floor to sit up. I wield the gun from my hip to eye level.

He won't change his mind.

I pull the trigger.

The bullet rips through Diego's shoulder. His chest flexes forward and he cries out before giving in to the pain and flopping against the floor.

"Fuck you, Victoria," he gasps.

My hand is shaking where before it was steady. I wipe a tear from my eye. No time to change my mind now.

I stick my gun back in its holster, stand, and grab Diego's gun from the floor. I latch the safety and thrust it down my back as I watch a pool of blood form around my lover from the mess that I created. I know I don't have a lot of time…

Vicente nods in approval.

THIRTEEN

A pair of loose faded jeans lies on the edge of the bed. The kind so well-worn with memories you wouldn't dare throw them out. I slip them over my black bikini bottoms and walk along an old plank floor towards an even older-looking window structure. Along the way, I grab a white cotton blouse and throw it over my shoulders.

This place…with its sparse, rustic furniture, its white-washed walls, a few hand-painted murals to evoke the folklore of the region…it soothes my restless mind.

I place a palm against the window frame as a breeze rustles the curtains. It's fall, so the current is crisp and refreshing, hardening my nipples. My lungs fill with air laced with moisture from the Adriatic Sea. Seagulls squawk overhead.

I lean forward so that I can observe him.

This is where he went after leaving the hospital and disappearing from my radar. It seems so obvious now, but it took me some time to figure it out. The world is full of possibilities for a man like Diego.

They're still out there—Diego and his physical therapist. Really more a trainer, who shows little mercy as he yells for Diego to push harder. Diego rotates his shoulder upwards and bellows back…from the pain. Then he's transitioned to another exercise, switching from focused shoulder work to full-body isometrics.

They do this for at least a couple hours every day, wrapping up just before sunset. I've been watching them since my arrival a few days ago.

He's wearing bright orange sweatpants and no top, even though the temperature is cool this time of day. It pains me seeing his bandaged arm, knowing I caused that. And his beautiful torso, knowing I may never be able to touch it again.

His shoulder *is* healing faster than the doctor expected. By the time I'd dragged Diego into that twin engine and flown him to the nearest hospital in Miami, he'd lost a lot of blood and the bullet had created an infection. The first operation didn't go well, so the Herreras flew him back to their trusted specialist in Mexico City. He couldn't move his arm for weeks. So even though he had the best doctors working on him, I worried about his spirit depleting.

Then, one day, he was gone. He'd checked out of the hospital and none of my reconnaissance could uncover where he went to. It felt like losing Renaldo all over again. I couldn't eat or sleep.

Vicente and I were still on good terms—I'd called for help for him amidst rescuing Diego—but I decided to distance myself from his business. Possibly for good.

I'd found out more about the opiate shipments. José Herrera was at the center of them, but he'd also been blackmailed by people in the Moreno organization as soon as they figured out they could demand a hefty cut for their silence. I also discovered that as much as the Herreras viewed my relationship with Diego as a threat, so did Vicente to his organization.

I worried this was at the root of Diego's disappearance. If they couldn't kill me, or him, maybe they'd found a way to put distance between us, the way they had after high school.

The therapist is stretching Diego's shoulder backwards and Diego is yelling like he's taking down a bear. I wish it was me his yells were directed at, but I'm not sure he'll ever even talk to me again.

It's over, and Diego is panting. They shake hands and walk back to the café.

With Diego just two flights of stairs below me, my breathing hastens. I reach for my glass of water on the table and focus on the sun hovering over the horizon.

We didn't kill each other. He didn't kill Vicente, which would have started a witch hunt. And José is being proven wrong. With him dead, the drug operation is falling apart. At least in its current form. That must count for something.

Peace between the two families is a long way off but possible again, "as long as you and Diego stay apart." Those were Vicente's stern words after my mother's funeral. Maybe that's all I was ever meant to do…move on from this life my mother fashioned.

But I'm having a hard time moving on. The space between Diego and me, and the loss of my mother have made me acutely aware of the emptiness in my life. That's why I told Vicente I was leaving, indefinitely.

Diego is right. I've been in too deep. So even though this is the life my mother decided on for us, I need to blaze my own path. Like I always have.

Enough. I gulp down the last of my water and slam down the glass. I spin on my bare feet, yank a beach towel off its hook, and head for the door.

I know he'll be eating dinner with his therapist, going over the ground they've covered and what's left to do. Hungry from his workout, he'll be more focused on his food than on some lone stranger taking a sunset dip. At least that's what I've observed.

I'm not sure how long I can keep observing, or if I'll ever work up the courage to talk to him. He's probably better off without me. But I'm aching to share with him that I'm in touch with the family who took over our textile business after my mom and I fled South Africa. They were ecstatic to hear from me and I'm planning on visiting them. With more political stability now, maybe there's even a place for me after all these years, in the business my father built.

I shuffle quietly out of the building, and my feet hit the rocky beach. The irregular edges awaken my soles, and I know the cool water will do the same for the rest of me.

I stare out at the tide, the waves bigger now than they were midday.

"They've observed an unusually large school of pelagic stingrays in these waters, which haven't migrated yet. Some are still birthing. Their sting can be severe—even fatal."

The voice at my back is all too familiar. And correct.

I heard about the phenomenon a few days ago from locals. They blamed it on heavy fishing of the stingray's natural predators, causing an overpopulation that now lurked in shallower, warmer waters looking for additional prey. I'd decided to take my chances.

I turn to face him. My chest flutters. I can smell the dried sweat on his taut brown skin. I love that smell. I've missed that smell.

"Isn't that what you want?" I ask.

"I want you to stop trying to prove something."

He steps closer to me, the crunch of rocks under his feet filling my ears.

"The tide is high right now, and the waves are rough. The conditions are perfect for feeding."

I look at him, unblinking. "They haven't gotten me yet. I won't let them get me now." I pause. "There's too much at stake."

He carefully places one foot in front of the other.

"Once they get you with their sting…they'll wrap their pectoral fins around you and manipulate their mouth to cut into you with their pointed teeth—"

"You don't know that I won't be able to outswim them."

He grabs the edges of the towel around my neck and pulls me closer. Our skin is almost touching. Goosebumps form on my arms.

"Perra terca," he accuses.

As he fingers the folds in the towel, I bite at my lower lip. He crosses the terry cloth ends and pulls it tighter across my neck.

"Maybe you should try shooting them in the shoulder instead," he says.

I deserve that. Though I was trying to save him.

"Through the chest cavity if I want to send a permanent message," I clarify.

"Stubborn fucking bitch," he repeats—in English this time because he means it. He takes one more step towards me, his chest now pressed against the thin fabric covering my nipples. "Who I have finally walked away from."

Our chests heave in a rhythm fiercer than the waves slapping against the shore. He lets go of the towel.

"What are you doing here, Victoria?"

The wind at my back picks up, swirling my hair against the bandage across his shoulder.

"I wanted to make sure you were…alright."

He grits his teeth. "No. You wanted to relieve your guilt."

My stomach clenches. "If you never wanted me to find you, you wouldn't have come back here."

He hesitates. "You're right. I was hoping you'd come." He sticks one hand in the pocket of his sweats. "So that I could call my men and turn you over to them." He pulls out a cell phone, flexing his hand around the plastic case.

I step away from him. "I'm not the bad guy, Diego."

"Maybe not, but you always think you're killing a bad guy, like some kind of vigilante, and that's dangerous."

His phones starts ringing. This may indeed be another setup, and this time I'm not prepared. I'm completely at his mercy.

He glances at the number and then back at me, before shoving the phone back in his pocket.

"You're still trying to avenge your father, and you think you'll never make a mistake." His eyes bore into me. "José wasn't responsible for your mother's death."

I purse my lips. "I know, but *you* would have made a mistake killing Vicente," I counter, "and you know it. I didn't want you to pay for that mistake with your life." I reach my fingers towards the bandage. The coarse fabric is like razors against my skin. "I'm sorry."

He stops my hand and pulls away. I shouldn't have expected anything else, but if this is where our story ends, he needs to know…

"I told Vicente I was leaving. Maybe for good if the right situation—"

"And you've suddenly had an epiphany that I'm the right situation?" he cuts me off.

I want to tell him that he's all I've thought about since he disappeared. That I've memorized every angle and curve of his face, every edge and arc of his body. I can't get his voice out of my mind, laced with that sexy accent, telling me all the things he wants to do to me. Clinging to the memory of his arms wrapped around me is what allows me to slip away from all the bullshit in my head and in my life.

"We fit well. Together" is all I manage to say, and awkwardly. I've never been good at expression.

His fingers travel down the length of my jaw line and pause at my chin before dropping.

"What if we don't fit…well…anymore?"

He turns away from me and walks slowly towards the inn.

Trembling, I step out of my jeans and toss off my blouse. I bolt for the water.

My skin hitting the current is like a slap of reality. *How could I think this was going to be easy?* My strokes through the waves get more aggressive as I fight to get past the swell. I get pulled towards the shore but propel myself further away from it. When I finally reach the calm, my tired body floats on the surface as my mind settles into acceptance.

I messed up and now I have to move on from Diego and what could've been.

I kick backwards and arch my back, somersaulting under the water. In the distance is a cluster of triangular shadows… also wondering if I can outswim them.

FOURTEEN

Shivering, I walk through the café, ducking my head as I pass the few patrons, the waitress, the housekeeper who cleans the rooms, and…the owner.

Petra's silver-grey hair is pulled back in a loose bun. She has a black cardigan over her light frock. Our smiles are courteous as we near one another. She was surprised to see me when I first arrived but didn't pry.

She glances at the finger that had a ring on it the last time I was here.

"You still want to borrow plane?" she asks, gently placing a hand on my shoulder.

"Probably not," I reply, wanting to tell her so much more.

"Maybe card game?"

I nod. *I'd really like that.*

She pats my shoulder and continues walking.

Clutching the towel around my clothes like a cape, the wet bikini on my fingers bouncing against my chest, I hurry up the creaky stairs and down the hallway to the door of my room.

My hand shakes as I wrestle with the lock, until the key slides in and clicks.

"I want to show you something."

I freeze as I'm about to push open the door, and turn around instead.

Diego's head is now covered with a hoodie. He motions for me to follow him.

I barely have the wherewithal to retrieve my key before shuffling behind him, trying not to show too much enthusiasm. Down the hallway and up another flight of stairs, we reach a set of double doors.

He turns the knob very carefully, because he knows the implications of crossing this threshold, again.

My chest heaves as the door closes behind us. It's the room we stayed in together when we tried to escape reality the first time. I recognize the slanted ceiling over the bed and the long windows, almost the size of French doors, that lead to a shallow balcony.

Damp wood penetrates my nostrils as my ears fill with the cry of seagulls and the crashing of waves. The flapping wings of a moth hovering near my face adds to the sensory input, which heightens as he walks over to the desk and picks up a folder.

"Renaldo was murdered." He hands me the thick file. "But not by my hand."

The words peel open a wound that I didn't expect to think about tonight.

"Wha—?" I stutter. "I mean, why did it take so long—"

"The information you're holding…it exposes corruption at the highest levels of FIFA." He shuts a window and pulls back his hoodie. "They weren't supposed to win the World Cup."

Dropping my bikini and towel, I thumb through the pages, catching sight of some key words…*gambling, embezzlement, money laundering, Secretary General, media rights…*

"What's being done about it?"

"This would be a public relations nightmare. I know FIFA is planning on ousting their president. They have to be very careful. Billions are at stake."

Part of me wants to run away, while the other part wants to scream in horror that Renaldo died over the financial interests of the corporate elite.

I put a hand to my mouth. "One person getting fired doesn't feel like justice."

He starts to respond, but stops, shaking his head and throwing me a fresh towel.

"I just wanted you to know that it wasn't me. Or my family."

I drop the heavy file to the floor and catch the dry towel, shoving it between my knees.

"That's it?" I ask, now flinging off everything damp, including the jeans I step out of like a dare, clutching the towel to my bare chest.

He circles me and drags a finger down my spine pensively.

"Bonita," he whispers, sending a shiver along the length of my skin. And then, "Drop to your knees."

He issues his command like someone who recognizes the power balance has shifted in their favor.

I hesitate.

"My suite, my rules, right?"

It's not really a question—just a rhetorical reiteration of how we've been playing our game.

I do as he asks, lowering myself slowly and deliberately, and then planting my hands on the ground long enough to let him take in the view of me arching on all fours before straightening to his waist level.

When he walks in front of me, I see the bulge in his pants and stifle a smile.

His hands land in my windswept hair and gently massage my scalp before firmly tugging my hair towards his growing erection. My knees stutter-step on the hard wood to keep up with his demand.

I grip the edges of his sweatpants, my mouth opening before his magnificent cock is even revealed. My lips land on the soft hairs of his happy trail, asking for forgiveness without uttering a word.

"Take it in your mouth."

I pull his elastic waistband down below his hardness and slowly run my tongue across the shaft, tasting it like a fine whiskey whose nuanced flavors are meant to be savored.

Except I want more than just a taste.

He moans when I swallow it, so deep it almost chokes me, wanting it to leave a permanent mark, just like the ring has. Bobbing up and down, I suck harder every time my head rises and drops, my other hand grasping his weighty balls.

"Holy shit, baby," he murmurs. "Slow down."

But I ignore him, pumping like a woman whose been denied for way too long.

He grabs a crop of my hair again and pulls hard enough for me to take notice. I release him and look up, mouth foaming, eyes watering.

He guides me, still by the crop of hair, up and over to the bed, smacking my ass hard as I fall over the thin mattress. He hovers over me, his stiff cock right at my opening, then his fingers maneuver around my thighs until they're pressing on my pussy. I groan, pushing back and grinding until everything is as slippery as a winding road after a rainstorm.

"I can walk away," he grunts in my ear, struggling to balance with his bad shoulder. "Even right now—as much as I want to slide inside of you and feel that tight pussy clench around me."

His thumb glides over my clit and I whimper.

"Yes," he replies to my appeal. "Slowly at first, and then faster, until you're at the edge, and I slow down to make sure you feel every inch of me inside of you when you're coming."

He pumps against my ass cheeks to the rhythm of his words, continuing to work my sensitive nub. I'm quivering, the heat spreading and my insides clenching as I near the orgasm I've been fantasizing about for months.

He pulls his fingers away and my body grinds to an unbearable halt.

"If you're fucking with me, or trying to pull something over me, I swear to god, Victoria, you will never see me again."

I know he's serious. We've been to this brink too many times. Some might call it unfair.

But then, very few things in life are fair.

"I'm not." I'm panting like I'm about to hyperventilate, but my mind is clear. "This is what I want, Diego. Every day.

All the time, until…I don't know." My body is dripping and twisting beneath him.

He straightens to relieve the pressure on his shoulder. "Tilt up. Your ass."

I do as he says, as if my whole future depends on it, my toes gripping the floor to provide leverage.

His left palm plants on my rear, now angled enough for him to observe my opening, while his right hand guides his cock an inch into my swollen lips. I moan with relief as he continues to enter me, breaking apart any last bit of doubt that I had about being here.

I feel him all the way in. Engorged inside of me. His cock throbs as his hands grip my hips to pump in and out, his balls slapping against my rear, slowly at first and then faster, until I quietly wail, feeling a climax building.

Then he slows, just like he said he would.

"I want you to explode all over my cock, but I want you to promise me something first."

His hands move down my thighs as his teeth bite into the back of my neck. It only makes me more eager. He knows damn well he has me where he wants me right now in any negotiation.

"You're incorrigible."

His fingers move to play with my clit again.

"This is what I want, too. Every day. All the time, until… you don't know, but I do." His cock throbs. "Forever. Not maybe, but forever. I want you to be mine, Victoria. I want you to marry me."

I can barely register the words, but I don't delay the answer.

"Yes," I yelp out as a climax roars to life from deep within. "Yes, yes, yes…" I repeat, clenching around his cock as he starts pumping into me again.

"Ven por mi, de nuevo. Ven sobre mi," he says, reaching his arms above me.

I've missed that dirty talk.

He cups one breast and rubs a finger over my responsive nipple as my other breast rubs against the thin sheets beneath me. I bear down on his cock, flexing around it as it pulses. I build just the right amount of pressure to come a second time, which always has more intensity.

Just as I begin to tremor, I feel him do the same. He groans as he strains to drive deeper, until we both collapse, barely hanging on to the flimsy sheets on the bed.

The room is silent, except for our breaths, huffing briefly in unison before each syncopates to its own rhythm.

He pulls out of me and flops onto the mattress, grabbing a pillow to prop up his injured shoulder.

I heave myself up next to him.

The bandage has loosened, and I give it an extra tug to unravel the remainder.

Gazing at his scar, I place my fingers over the bullet hole I created.

There's no turning back now.

Photo: Raphael Rogers

S.L. Hannah was born in Poland, grew up in Canada, and moved to Southern California to pursue her love of single-engine airplanes. *Hard Trigger* is her sixth book, and her first "rogue romance." Visit her online at **www.slhannah.com** to get updates about her next book, and to connect through social media.

S.L. Hannah lives in Los Angeles, California, with her husband, her garden of succulents, and her feisty little dog-boss. When she's not writing fiction, she continues to solve the aviation problems of the world.

LETTER FROM THE AUTHOR

Dear Reader,

First of all, thank you! Writing a book is an incredibly emotional journey. And after all the research and editing followed by feedback from beta readers followed by more editing, it is a thrill to finally be able to share this story with you. But the journey doesn't end once a book is published. It is truly another beginning.

As an author, your greatest hope is for the journey to continue, as the story lingers in the minds and hearts of your readers. You seek to inspire their own soul-searching, as well as conversations about your book with their friends and friends of friends.

You can help me keep that dialogue going by reviewing this book online—on Amazon, Goodreads, Kobo, the iBookstore, Barnes & Noble, and/or Shelfari. Your words and ratings on those platforms really do make a difference and help me stay writing as an author.

Hard Trigger is an action-packed adventure full of hot relationship drama—one that started out as a short story and then took on a life of its own. But I have always been driven to tell stories from a strong female point of view that exposes the strength of my gender. And I have always wanted to write a female James Bond–type character. Sexy, savvy, intense, and unapologetic. I hope this book strikes a chord...

Thank you so much for your continued support.

xoxoxox,

Hannah

READER DISCUSSION QUESTIONS

1. Is it a risk, emotional or otherwise, for Victoria to marry Diego, and will the Herreras truly accept her?

2. Will Victoria be able to subdue her killer instinct?

3. Will Diego be able to leave his family and Mexico City for a life in South Africa?

4. Will Victoria's loyalty to Vicente bring her back to Mexico City?

5. How did Victoria's poker savvy help her stay alive?

6. Will the opiate business that José started find new life due to demand and once again impact the Herrera-Moreno relationship?

7. Should we legalize all drugs to thwart the criminal activity tied to them?

8. Whose guns laws are more strict: Mexico's or the United States'?

9. Can and should Diego and Victoria ever truly trust one another?

10. Do Diego and Victoria have a chance at a happily-ever-after?

What do you think?

Let me know by connecting with me on Goodreads and starting a discussion: https://www.goodreads.com/sl_hannah

CONNECT WITH ME

If you are interested in reading my future books, please sign up for my newsletter and exclusive offers at: www.slhannah.com. In the meantime, check out *The Need*, my wild and thought-provoking erotic thriller, and stay tuned for my next book, *Open Endings*, which will be just as provocative.

My alternate-genre publications, include my acclaimed chick-lit series, *Sex, Life, and Hannah*, and my foray into a dark fairytale world with the award-winning *The Dentist and the Toothfairy*.

On Social Media:

www.goodreads.com/sl_hannah

www.facebook.com/sexlifeandhannah

www.twitter.com/sexlifehannah

www.instagram/sexlifehannah

Author websites:

www.slhannah.com

www.sexlifeandhannah.com

www.thedentistandthetoothfairy.com

www.ingramcontent.com/pod-product-compliance
Lightning Source LLC
Chambersburg PA
CBHW051841170626
46807CB00003B/1293